This was it.

The challenge that was going to tell him who he really was. What his values really were and whether he was made of the right stuff to rule a country in the best interests of the many thousands of people who would be trusting him to do the right thing.

He'd convinced himself that resisting the attraction he felt toward Mika was that test, so why—in this moment after those words had been uttered, and it felt like time was holding its breath—did it feel so utterly *wrong*?

As if he didn't really have a choice at all?

Again, he was reminded of when she had taken his hand, up there on top of that cliff. Of when her trembling had finally ceased and he'd known she was trusting him.

He'd felt taller, then. Powerful in a way that had nothing to do with him as a prince but everything to do with who he was as a man. Nothing would have persuaded him to break that trust.

And right now Mika was trusting him with so much more than her hand. She was asking him to take hold of her whole body and, by doing so, he would still be leading her to safety—wouldn't he?

Dear Reader,

One of the best things about being a writer is that when life throws tough stuff at you, there's a little voice in the back of your head that says, "You can *so* use this in a book..."

And it was exactly one of those moments that gave me the start of this story...

A few years ago I was lucky enough to spend a few days with a writer friend of mine, doing a walking tour of the Amalfi Coast in Italy. There I was, thousands of feet up on the side of a mountain, only to discover—to my horror—that I can suffer from vertigo. I had no idea how debilitating—and terrifying—it can be!

On the plus side, I also got to remember how magical so many other things were about that trip, and I could revel in every one of them as I wove them into this story. And for the bits I didn't know about—well, I had the joy of picking my daughter's brain about her extensive experience working in the hospitality industry, which engendered both laughter and sympathy.

I love this story for its setting and I love both Mika and Raoul for what they learn about life and find in each other.

I hope you do, too.

With love,

Alison xxx

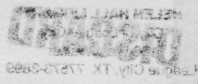

The Forbidden Prince

—

Alison Roberts

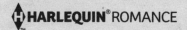

H HARLEQUIN® ROMANCE

Recycling programs
for this product may
not exist in your area.

ISBN-13: 978-0-373-74398-8

The Forbidden Prince

First North American publication 2016

Printed in U.S.A.

Alison Roberts is a New Zealander, currently lucky enough to live near a beautiful beach in Auckland. She is also lucky enough to write for both the Harlequin Romance and Medical Romance lines. A primary schoolteacher in a former life, she is also a qualified paramedic. She loves to travel and dance, drink champagne and spend time with her daughter and her friends.

Books by Alison Roberts

Harlequin Romance

The Logan Twins

The Maverick Millionaire

In Her Rival's Arms
The Wedding Planner and the CEO
The Baby Who Saved Christmas

Visit the Author Profile page
at Harlequin.com for more titles.

For Becky

With all my love

CHAPTER ONE

So THIS WAS what freedom felt like.

Raoul de Poitier sucked in a deep breath as he paused to get his first proper glimpse of the view he'd climbed about two thousand steps to find.

He had the whole world at his feet.

Well…he had what looked like a large part of the Amalfi coast of the Mediterranean down there, anyway. Far, far below he could pick out the tiny blue patch that was the swimming pool on the roof of the hotel Tramonto d'Oro where he'd stayed last night. Beside that was the tiled dome and spire of the ancient church against the terracotta tiles and white houses of the small coastal town of Praiano.

Beyond the village, the waters of the Mediterranean stretched as far as the horizon, a breathtakingly sapphire blue as the sunlight gentled its way to dusk. Somewhere out there was his homeland—the European principality of *Les Iles Dauphins*.

Another deep breath was released in what felt like a sigh, and with it came a pang of... what... homesickness? Guilt, perhaps?

His grandfather was ill. His heart was failing and it was time for him to step down from ruling his land. To hand the responsibility to the next-in-line to the throne.

His grandmother would be anxious. Not only about her beloved husband but about the grandson she'd raised as her own child after the tragic death of his parents.

'I don't understand, Raoul. A holiday...yes. Time to prepare yourself for what is to come. For your marriage... But alone? Incognito? That's not who you are.'

'Maybe that's what I need to find out, Mamé. And this is the last chance I will ever get.'

No. The pang wasn't guilt. He needed this time to centre himself for what was to come. To be sure that he had what it took to put aside his own desires if that was what was required to protect and nurture a whole nation, albeit a tiny one. He was thirty-two years old but he hadn't been really tested yet. Oh, there'd been formal duties that had got in the way of private pleasures, and he had always had to curb any desire to push the boundaries of behaviour that might be frowned on by others. But, within that reasonably relaxed circumference, he'd been able to achieve the career that had been top of his chosen list—as a helicopter pilot in his country's first-rate rescue service. And he'd had his share of a seemingly infinite supply of beautiful women.

All that was about to change, however. The boundaries would shrink to contain him in a very tight space. Almost every minute of every day would be accounted for.

He had always known it would happen. He just wasn't sure how ready he was to accept it. Somehow, he needed to find that out. To test himself, by himself, which was why this had to be in a place where he knew no one and no one knew who he was.

Was it homesickness, perhaps? Because he was feeling a new and rather extraordinary sensation of being alone? No. He'd dealt with homesickness many years ago when he'd been sent to the best schools that Europe had to offer and, while the love of his family and homeland would always draw him back and enfold him, he loved to travel.

It was relief, that was what it was. He had won this time. A reprieve from thinking about the overwhelming responsibility of being in charge of a nation, along with the daunting prospect of a marriage that had been arranged when he'd been no more than a child. A union that would bond two similar principalities together and strengthen them both.

Raoul turned away from the view of the sea. Les Iles Dauphins was out of sight and he was going to try and put it out of mind for just a little while.

He was free. All he had was in his backpack and he could choose any direction at all, the time he would take to get there and how long he would stay when he did. As of yesterday, nobody knew where he was and he was confident that nobody would recognise him. His hair grew fast and he'd deliberately missed his last cut. His beard was coming along well, too. With his dark sunglasses, he could pass for any European tourist. Italian, French... Spanish, even.

He could feel the corners of his mouth curve. If he'd had a guitar case on his back instead of his backpack, he would probably have looked like a flashback to the sixties. He was completely alone for what felt like the first time in his entire life. No family, no friends and, most importantly, no bodyguards or lurking paparazzi. He had won the freedom simply to be himself.

He just needed to find out who that was, exactly, because he had a feeling there were layers to his personality that had been buried for ever. Even his earliest memories involved a performance of some kind. Of behaving in a way that would never have been expected of others.

How many five-year-olds could take part in a national ceremony to mourn both parents and not cry until they were finally alone in their own beds and presumed to be sound asleep? Who had childhood friends chosen for them and, even then, had to be careful of what was said? What young adult knew how much had been sacrificed by a generation that had already raised a child and shouldn't have had to start all over again? The burden of a debt that could never properly be repaid had never been intended but it was there all the same.

He had never been drunk enough to do anything inappropriate or create a scandal by dating indiscreet women. He had excelled in his university studies and military training and, until he'd taken this leave, had shone in his role as a helicopter pilot for a service that provided both military transport and emergency rescue services.

Sometimes, it felt like his life had been recorded by photographs that had been staged for public consumption and approval. A picture-perfect life of a happy prince. And the next album would have all the pomp and ceremony of his coronation, then his wedding and then the births of the next generation of the de Poitier royal family.

The happiness was not an illusion. Raoul loved his life and knew how incredibly fortunate he was but his curiosity of the unknown had teased him with increasing frequency of late. Was there something solid that formed the essence of who he was as a person? Something that would have been there if he hadn't been born a prince?

He had four weeks to try and find some kind of answer to what seemed an impossible question and the only plan he had come up with was to see if he could find a challenge that would be testing enough to make him dig deep. He had set out with no more than the bare essentials of survival in a backpack—a phone, a fake ID, limited funds and a change of clothes. This demanding climb up a mountain to the track that led from Praiano to Positano was just the first step on a very private journey.

Or maybe it wasn't quite that private.

Frowning, Raoul stared at the narrow, winding track ahead of him. He could hear voices. One voice, anyway.

Faint.

Female.

'Aiuti... Per favore aiutatemi...'

The vertigo had come from nowhere.

Utterly unexpected and totally debilitating.

Tamika Gordon was clinging to the side of a cliff and she didn't dare open her eyes. If she did, the nausea would come back, the world would start spinning again and there would be nothing to stop her falling into that terrifyingly sheer drop onto rocks hundreds of feet below. But keeping her eyes shut didn't wipe out the knowledge that the unprotected edge to this track was no more than the length of her arm away.

The panic that led her to cry for help was almost as terrifying as the yawning chasm below.

Mika didn't do panic. She'd been told more

than once that she was 'as hard as nails' and she was proud of it. It was a badge of honour, won by surviving. Of course she was tough. Who wouldn't be when they'd been dragged up through a succession of disastrous foster homes and then had ended up on the streets as a teenager? She'd fought for everything she had achieved in her twenty-nine years on earth so far and she'd been confident she could cope with whatever life chose to throw at her.

But this…this was totally out of her control. She'd fought it for as long as possible with sheer willpower but the symptoms were physical rather than mental and they had increased in ferocity until she'd reached a point of complete helplessness—reduced to a shivering blob of humanity clinging to a couple of tufts of coarse mountain grass. It was beyond humiliating. She'd be angry about it as soon as she got out of this and the terror had a chance to wear off. *If* she ever got out of this…

She hadn't seen anyone else on this supposedly popular walking route so far. Maybe that was her own fault. She'd chosen to set off from Praiano much later in the day than most people because she knew the light would be so much better for taking photographs. And maybe she'd spent too much time down at the monastery halfway up the steps, taking photographs with her precious new camera and scribbling notes in her pristine journal.

How long would it be before it got dark?

'*Help…*' She tried English this time instead of Italian. 'Can anyone hear me?'

Her voice wavered and tears stung as they gathered behind her eyelids. This recognition of a despair she hadn't felt since she'd been too young to protect herself had to be the worst moment of her adult life.

'I'm coming… Hold on…'

She wasn't alone. There was hope to be found now. A glowing light in the darkness of that despair. It was a male voice she'd heard, the words short, as if he was out of breath, and in the space after those words Mika could hear the sound of shoes crunching on the sparse gravel of the track.

He was *running*?

When there were only a few feet between the steep wall of the cliff above and that appalling drop into nothingness below?

The speed of the footsteps slowed and then stopped.

'What is it?' A deep voice with a faint accent that she couldn't place. 'Are you hurt?'

Mika shook her head, her eyes still tightly closed. The overwhelming relief at not being alone any more made speech impossible for several breaths.

'Vertigo,' she managed finally, hating how pathetic her voice sounded. 'I... I can't move...'

'You're safe,' the man said. 'I'll keep you safe.'

Dear Lord...had anybody *ever* said that to her? Being so helpless had made her feel like a small child again, so it was too easy to imagine how it would feel to have somebody say those words to that frightened little girl. To feel fear and desolation start to drain away as if a plug had been pulled. To have an insight into how different her life might have been if somebody had said that to her, back then, and meant it. If somebody had been there to protect her. To love her...

How humiliating was it to have her outward breath sound like a child's sob? She'd learned long ago that weakness was something to be hidden very deeply.

'It's okay,' the man said. 'You're going to be fine. How long have you been stuck?'

'I…don't know.' It felt like for ever.

'Are you thirsty? I have water.'

She heard a shuffling sound and then a zip opening. She was thirsty but to accept a water bottle would mean opening her eyes, and what if the spinning started again? Sobbing in front of a stranger was bad enough. Imagine if she threw up?

'It's okay. I don't need a drink.'

There was a moment's silence. 'What's your name?'

'Mika.'

'It's a pleasure to meet you, Mika.'

This time her breath came out as a huff of something closer to laughter than tears. Her rescuer had very nice manners. He sounded as though they'd just been introduced at a cocktail party.

'I'm Ra…um… Rafe.'

She had only been speaking to him for a minute or two, and she didn't even have any idea what he looked like, but the hesitation seemed out of character. Did he not want her to know his real name? Was it possible that she was about to step from the frying pan into the fire and put her faith in an axe murderer? Or a…a rapist?

It might have been five years ago but the fear was always too close to the surface. If he hadn't chosen that precise moment to touch her, she could have dealt with it. It wasn't like the vertigo; she could persuade herself to think rationally and conquer it.

But he touched her arm and moving away from that touch was too instinctive to avoid. Mika let go of her tufts of grass with every intention of trying to run but her legs were still shaking and she lost her footing. Desperately trying to stop the skid, she reached for the grass again, but it slid through her fingers. Her foot made contact with something solid and she pushed against it but that, too, slid out of touch. She landed on her hands and knees, aware of a sound like rocks falling that provided a background to the soft but vehement curse that came from her rescuer.

And then silence.

Cautiously, Mika sat back on her heels as she tried to process what had just happened.

'Are you all right?'

'Yes. I'm sorry. I… I slipped.'

'Hmm…'

She could feel him watching her. 'Did I… um…kick you?'

'No. You kicked my backpack. It went over the cliff.'

Mika's eyes opened smartly. '*What?* Oh, no... I'm *so* sorry...'

'Better the pack than you.'

It seemed extraordinary but he was smiling at her. A smile that made the corners of his eyes crinkle. Dark eyes. Dark, shaggy hair and a dark jaw that had gone well past designer stubble but wasn't quite a beard. And he was big. Even crouching he seemed to tower over her.

Weird that the fear that had prompted this unfortunate development was ebbing away instead of increasing. Maybe it was those eyes. This man might be in a position of power over her right now but he wasn't any kind of predator. He looked...nice. Kind?

You're safe. I'll keep you safe.

'Did it have anything important in it? Like your wallet?' A churning in her stomach reminded her not to try looking over the edge of the cliff.

'There's no point worrying about that right now. The light's going to fade before long, Mika. I need to get you off this track.'

Mika nodded. She scrambled to her feet, her own light pack still secure on her back. If she didn't look into the chasm, maybe she would be okay. She looked towards the solid side of the cliff, reaching out her hand to touch it as well.

'I'm trying to decide which way would be best. You've come a long way onto the open part of the track already. It's probably better to keep going towards Positano rather than go down all those steps when it's getting darker.'

Mika swallowed hard and then nodded again. 'That's where I'm living at the moment. In Positano.'

'The track is quite narrow. Do you want me to walk ahead of you or behind?'

'Ahead, I think… I can watch your feet. If I don't look at the drop, maybe the dizziness won't come back.'

It worked…for a little while…but, try as she might, Mika became more and more aware of the emptiness on the left side in her peripheral vision. Using her free hand to provide a kind of blinker also helped for a while but it wasn't enough. Her stomach began to fold itself into spasms of distress and her brain began a slow, sickening spin. She tried to focus on the boots in front of her: smart, expensive-looking leather hiking boots. Thick socks were rolled down above them and then there were bare legs, muscles under olive skin outlined with every step.

'How's it going?'

Mika dropped the hand she was using as a shield to look up as Raoul turned his head when she didn't respond immediately. She tried to smile but changing the focus of her vision seemed to have made the spinning sensation worse.

'Here… It might help to hold my hand.'

It was there, right in front of her, palm downwards and fingers outstretched in invitation.

And it was huge.

Not the hand, although it had long, artistic-looking fingers. No. It was the idea of voluntarily putting her own into it that was so huge. Five years was a very long time not to have allowed the touch of a man's skin against her own.

But the need to survive was an overwhelmingly strong motivation. Strong enough to break a protective barrier that was inappropriate in this moment. She put her hand in his and felt his fingers curl around hers. She could feel the strength of the arm attached to that hand. The solidity of the body attached to the arm. The confidence of each step that was being taken.

He was half a pace ahead of her, because there was no room to walk side by side, but the hand was all that mattered.

He was holding her.

And he would keep her safe.

She was a fighter, this Mika.

And there was something wild about her.

She was certainly unlike any woman he'd ever met before. For a start, she was out here all by herself, which advertised independence and courage, but she was tiny. Her head barely reached his shoulder, which probably made her look younger than she really was—an intriguing contrast to those big, dark eyes that made you think she'd seen far more than her age should have allowed for. She had spiky dark hair, which should have seemed unattractive to someone who'd always favoured long, blonde tresses, but he had to admit that it suited Mika. So did the clothes that looked more suitable for a walk on a beach than a mountain hike— denim shorts that were frayed at the bottom and a loose white singlet, the hem of which didn't quite meet the waistband of the shorts.

The shoes weren't exactly suitable either, being well-worn-looking trainers, and it looked as though her feet were bare inside them, but the surprise of that choice had been well and truly surpassed when Raoul had noticed her tattoo. The inked design looked tribal—like a series of peaked waves encircling her upper arm just below armpit level. No. Maybe even that observation had been trumped by spotting the tiny charm on the simple silver chain around her neck.

A dolphin…

The symbol of his homeland. What would she think if she knew that she was wearing something that gave her an instant connection to everything he held most dear in his life?

But it had been that instinctive flinch from a touch that had been intended as no more than reassurance that had really given him the sense of wildness about her. It wasn't just the physical appearance that said she made her own choices or the fact that she was alone in a potentially dangerous place. It was that wariness of the touch, the hesitation in accepting contact from another human, that had been revealed by her body language when he'd offered to take her hand.

The trembling he'd felt when she'd finally accepted the offer.

Or perhaps it was the way she'd been doggedly following him even though it was clearly an enormous struggle. She'd been as white as a sheet when he'd turned to check on how she was doing. He could see that she was pushing herself beyond her limits but he could also see the determination that she wasn't going to let it defeat her. Anger, almost, that she'd been beaten into submission. Like a wild creature that had been trapped?

Another hundred metres along this goat track of a path—past a rustic wooden sign with Praiano written on one side and Nocelle on the other—and Raoul could feel that the trembling in her hand had ebbed. The holding had all been on his part to begin with but now he could feel a return pressure from that small hand he was holding and it made him feel…good.

Protective. She hadn't wanted him to touch her but she'd allowed it when she'd reached the end of her endurance.

She was trusting him and he wasn't going to break that trust. He would look after this wild creature of a woman until he was absolutely sure she was okay.

'Don't worry,' he told her. 'It'll wear off as soon as you don't have that drop beside you.'

'I know.' It sounded like she was speaking through gritted teeth.

'It's nothing to be ashamed of,' he added. 'Vertigo is like altitude sickness. It makes no difference how fit or strong you are. These things just happen.'

A tiny huff of sound suggested that Mika didn't let things just happen to *her* and Raoul felt a flash of empathy. Imagine if it had happened to him. If he'd set out to discover the qualities in himself that would allow him to face his future with confidence and he'd been left helpless and totally dependent on the kindness of a stranger...

Oddly, he felt almost envious of Mika. Maybe it took something that dramatic to strip away every layer that life had cloaked you with. To face that kind of fear would certainly reveal any strengths or weaknesses. Maybe the kind of challenge he needed was something like Mika had just faced—something that you would never choose voluntarily.

But you couldn't create one. Like the vertigo he'd told her about, it either happened or it didn't.

He *was* facing an unexpected development, however—a small thing, compared to Mika's challenge, but how on earth was he going to cope with losing that backpack? The clothing and toiletries didn't matter but he'd lost his wallet, passport and phone. It would be easy enough to place a call from a public telephone to request help but, even if his grandmother said nothing, he would hear the subtext of 'I told you so'. Going incognito to be a nobody in the real world was not something a prince should do. It wasn't who he was.

Failure wasn't an option. He just needed to come up with a new plan. Maybe he'd find inspiration by the time this walk was over.

The sigh he blocked after a few minutes of nothing remotely inspirational occurring seemed to transfer itself to Mika, as she pulled her hand from his.

'I'm okay now.'

He'd been so lost in his thoughts that Raoul hadn't noticed how the track had changed. They weren't on a cliff edge any more. The path had widened and there were trees on either side.

A glance at Mika and the change he saw in her appearance was startling. She was still pale but the tension in her face and the panic in her eyes had gone. And, if that hadn't made her look different enough, her mouthed curved into a grin that he could only describe as cheeky.

'Stupid, huh?'

It was impossible not to grin back.

'Not at all. Like I said, it can happen to anybody.'

'It's like a switch has been flicked off. Now that I can't see the cliff, I'm fine.' She ducked her head and when she looked up again there was something soft in her eyes. Something that made Raoul feel a flush of warmth like the tingle you got when you held cold hands out to a fire.

'Thank you *so* much. I… I think you might have saved my life.'

'It was my pleasure.' The words were quiet but he meant every one of them. Oddly, he needed to clear his throat after he'd uttered them. 'Let's hope there are no more open parts to the track.'

'I don't think there are. We should get to the village of Nocelle soon and then it's just a whole lot more steps down into Positano.' Mika raised her eyebrows. 'I wonder if the police station will still be open.'

'Excuse me?'

'So you can report the loss of your backpack. In case someone finds it.'

'I think that's highly unlikely. It didn't look like the kind of cliff anyone would be climbing for fun.'

'I can't believe I did that. I feel awful.'

'It doesn't matter. Really…'

For a few moments they walked in silence. Dusk was really gathering now, and it was darker amongst the trees, so coming across a small herd of goats startled them both. The goats were even more startled and leapt off the track to scramble up through the forest, the sound of their bleating and bells astonishingly loud in the evening stillness.

'Sorry, goats,' Mika called, but she was laughing. She even had some colour in her cheeks when she turned towards Raoul. 'I *love* Italy,' she told him. 'I might live here for ever.'

'Oh? You're not Italian, then?'

'Huh? We've been talking English since we met. What makes you think I'm Italian?'

'When I first heard you call for help, you spoke in Italian. And you've got a funny accent when you speak English.'

'I do *not*.' Mika sounded offended. 'I can

get by in Italian pretty well but English is my first language.'

'So you are from England?'

'No. I'm half-Maori, half-Scottish.'

'You don't *sound* Scottish.'

'I'm not. I'm a Kiwi.'

Raoul shook his head. She was talking in riddles. Her smile suggested she was taking pity on him.

'I come from New Zealand. Little country? At the bottom of the world?'

'Oh…of course. I know it. I've seen the *Lord of the Rings* movies. It's very beautiful.'

'It is. What about you, Rafe?'

'What about me?' He was suddenly wary.

'Rafe isn't your *real* name, is it?'

The wariness kicked up a notch. 'What makes you say that?'

'You sounded like you were going to say something else when you introduced yourself, that's all. Do you have a weird name or something?' That cheeky grin flashed again. 'Is Rafe short for Raphael?'

Relief that he hadn't been unexpectedly recognised made him chuckle. 'Um…something like that.'

'Rafe it is, then. Are *you* Italian?'

'No.'

'How come you speak English with a funny accent, then?'

He had to laugh again. 'I'm European. I speak several languages. My accent is never perfect.'

'It's actually pretty good.' The concession felt like high praise. 'Are you here on holiday?'

'Yes. You?'

'No, I'm working. I'm doing my OE.'

'Oh-ee?' The word was unfamiliar.

'Overseas Experience. It's a rite of passage for young New Zealanders.'

'Oh…and is it something you have to do alone?'

'Not necessarily.'

'But *you* are doing it alone?'

'Yep.' Her tone suggested she wouldn't welcome any further questions about her personal life. 'Oh, look—civilisation.'

Sure enough, they had reached the outskirts of the mountain village. There was no real reason to stay with Mika any longer. She had completely recovered and she was safe. But Raoul was enjoying her company now and he had to admit he was curious. Mika was a world away from her homeland and she was alone.

Why?

They walked in silence for a while as they entered the village of Nocelle. Raoul's eye was caught by big terracotta pots with red geraniums beneath a wooden sign hanging from a wrought-iron bar advertising this to be the Santa Croce *ristorante* and bar. Extending an invitation was automatic.

'Can I buy you a coffee or something to eat? I don't know about you, but I'm starving after that hike. We could get a bus down to Positano if it's too dark to use the steps later.'

The invitation had been impulsive—a polite thing for a gentleman to do. It was only after he'd voiced it that Raoul realised how much he actually wanted Mika to agree.

He wanted to offer her food, not just because he was reluctant to give up her company—he wanted to look after her for a little while longer. To recapture that heart-warming sensation of winning the trust of somebody who needed his help although they would have preferred not to accept it.

It was just to make absolutely sure she was okay, of course. Nothing more. Hooking up with any young woman on this trip was an absolute no-no and, besides, he'd never be physically attracted to somebody like Mika. She was a tomboy, possibly the complete opposite to any woman he'd ever invited into his life or his bed—those picture-perfect blondes that knew how to pose for an unexpected photograph. Maybe that explained the fascination.

She was looking almost as wary as she had when he'd offered his hand to help her along the track and suddenly—to his horror—Raoul realised it might be better if she declined the invitation. He could feel the smile on his face freeze as he discreetly tried to pat the pocket on his shorts. He might have enough loose change to cover a bus fare for them both but it was highly unlikely that he could pay for a meal.

He was still smiling but Mika seemed to be reading his mind. A furrow appeared on her forehead.

'Your wallet *was* in your backpack, wasn't it? You don't have any money, do you?'

'Ah…'

'What about your passport? And do you even have a place to stay?'

'Um…' The echo of the 'I told you so' vibe that he would very much prefer to avoid made him straighten his spine. 'I'll find somewhere.'

He found himself nodding. A short, decisive

movement. Maybe this unfortunate occurrence was actually a blessing in disguise. Exactly the kind of challenge he needed to find out what he was made of. Whether he could cope with a bit of genuine adversity.

'Do you have any friends around here?'

The nod morphed into a subtle shake, more of a head tilt, as the question unexpectedly captured Raoul on a deeper level. He'd never lacked for people desperate to be his friends but experience had taught him that it was all too often due to his position in life rather than any genuine personal connection. He was probably as wary of making friends as Mika was about letting someone offer her assistance. Of letting someone touch her. It was impossible to know, in fact, whether he had any real friends at all because he'd never been in this position before.

Being ordinary.

Meeting someone who was judging him on who he *really* was—as a man and not as a prince.

'Doesn't matter. You've got one now.' Mika's face lit up with that impish grin but it faded quickly to a much more serious expression. 'You saved my life, mate.' There was still a gleam in her eyes that didn't match her sombre expression. 'I'm afraid I can't subscribe to the Chinese tradition of becoming your slave for life to repay the debt but…' Her face scrunched into lines that suggested serious thought. 'But I can buy you dinner.' The grin flashed again. 'I might even splash out on a cold beer.'

Raoul couldn't take his eyes off Mika. Witnessing the confidence that was returning now that her frightening experience was over was like seeing a butterfly emerge from its chrysalis. The way her expressions changed so quickly, and the lilt of her voice with that unusual accent was enchanting, but perhaps the most extraordinary thing was the effect that smile had on him.

He wanted to see it again. To make her laugh, even…

And she'd declared herself to be his friend. Without having the faintest idea who he really was.

Oddly, that made him feel humble. It gave him a bit of lump in his throat, if he were honest.

'Come on, Raphael.' The pocket rocket that was his newest friend was already heading down the cobbled street towards the arched entrance to the restaurant. 'We'll eat and then we'll figure out what you're going to do. If you're starving, it's impossible to think about anything but food, don't you think?'

'Mmm...' But the lopsided grin—almost a wink—that had accompanied her use of what she thought was his real name made Raoul smile inwardly.

It was a rare experience indeed for him to be teased. He had no siblings, and apparently it hadn't been the done thing for others to tease a prince, even in childhood.

He liked it, he decided.

He liked Mika, too.

CHAPTER TWO

IT WAS ONE of the things that Mika loved about Italian villages—that she could rock up to a place like this, in shorts and a singlet top, probably looking as weary and in need of a shower as she felt, and still be welcomed with a smile and gestures that suggested they had been waiting for her arrival.

The change when Raoul entered the restaurant behind her was subtle but unmistakable. Instead of a welcome guest, Mika suddenly felt like a...*a princess*?

'This way, sir, please; this is the best seat in the house. And you're lucky. You get to catch the last of this magnificent sunset.'

The whole wall of the restaurant was glass and the building seemed to be perched on the side of the mountain. It was the same view they'd had from the top of the Footpath of the Gods, only now the Mediterranean was on fire with red and gold light, and the islands way up the coast were dark, mysterious humps. It was a similar drop over a cliff right beside them, too, with no more than a low, railed fence outside the window and a roof or two of houses well below on the steep slope.

The slight quirk of Rafe's eyebrow along with the expression in those dark eyes was remarkably eloquent. He wanted to know if she was okay to be sitting, overlooking the drop. He would be more than happy to forgo the view if she wasn't and he would request a change without embarrassing her by referring to her recent disability in public.

It made Mika feel even more like a princess.

No. It made her feel the same way that taking hold of his hand on the track had made her feel.

Protected.

Safe.

She had to clear her throat to get rid of an odd lumpy sensation before she spoke.

'This is gorgeous,' she said. 'Perfect.'

The white linen tablecloth was more of a worry than the view, in fact. Along with the silver cutlery, and the way their host flicked open a huge napkin and let it drape over her bare legs told Mika that this was nothing like the café she currently worked in. Was it going to be horrendously expensive? She remembered those nice boots Rafe was wearing. How well he spoke English when his accent advertised that it wasn't his first language. How the *maître d'* had instantly recognised somebody that deserved respect. Mika suspected that Rafe had come from a far more privileged background than hers. He was probably quite used to eating in restaurants that had linen tablecloths and silver cutlery.

Thank goodness she'd been paid yesterday.

'I will bring you the menu,' the *maître d'* said, reaching out to light the candle on their table. 'For drinks, also? We have a wide selection of the finest wines.'

It was Mika's turn to raise an eyebrow in Rafe's direction. At least, that was what she intended to do, but as soon as her gaze met his she completely forgot and found herself smiling instead. Was he as amused by this as she was? Here they were, looking like scruffy tourists, and they were being offered a selection of the finest wines.

'A glass of your house red, perhaps,' Rafe said.

'I'll have a beer, please,' Mika added. 'A really cold lager.'

With a nod, their waiter turned away. Mika glanced back at Rafe and this time her eyebrows did rise. He looked as though he was assessing something important. Something to do with herself? His face looked quite serious as he turned his head.

'Excuse me,' he called. 'I've changed my mind. Can you bring me a beer, too, please?'

It was a bit silly to feel so pleased about a simple change of drinks but it was as if Rafe was sealing their friendship in some way. Telling her that he liked her choice and was prepared to follow it.

She liked him, she decided. It was a bit disconcerting that merely his presence could alter an atmosphere in a room, as if he had an aura of some invisible power, but she didn't feel threatened by him in any way. Quite the opposite— and that was probably as disconcerting as how ridiculously good-looking that glow from the sunset through the window was making him seem.

Nobody was *that* perfect.

To cover the tumble of thoughts she had no intention of exploring, Mika opened her bag to take out her camera.

'I've got to get a photo of this sunset,' she told Rafe. 'How stunning is that?'

'It's amazing,' he agreed. 'I bet we could see as far as Capri in the day time.'

Mika wished she'd read more of the instruction booklet for her camera last night. She had to hope the settings were appropriate for the level of contrast out there.

'Nice camera,' Rafe said when she'd finished snapping.

'I know.' Mika sighed happily. 'It's a Nikon D4. Sixteen-point-two megapixels. It's my new baby,' she added quietly. 'I've been waiting a long time for this.' The first step to a new career. A new life.

'You're keen on photography?'

'Mmm.' Mika was scrolling through the photos she'd just taken. The dream of becoming a travel writer and supplying great photos to accompany her stories was too new and private to share. 'Look…' She tilted the screen of the camera towards Rafe. 'These are the ones I took of the monastery on the way up the mountain.'

He leaned forward and reached out to hold the other side of the camera as she kept scrolling.

'These are great. I just stopped long enough

to look at the view but you've captured so much more. That close-up of the stonework in the arch... And that hand-painted sign: *Convento San Domenico*,' he read aloud. '*Sentiero Degli Dei*.'

'Ah...you've walked our famous path.' The waiter delivered tall, frosty glasses filled with amber liquid. '*Sentiero Degli Dei*—Footpath of the Gods. It is beautiful, isn't it?'

'An experience I will remember for ever,' Mika answered truthfully.

Was the touch of Rafe's foot against hers under the table accidental? No. Judging by the gleam of mirth in his eyes, he was sharing a private understanding that the experience was not what the waiter might be assuming. It had been the lightest of touches...how come she could feel it all the way up her leg? Into an almost forgotten spot deep in her belly, even.

Mika put her camera down to pick up the menu that had come with the drinks. 'At least I got some good photos before it hit me. And I have my notes.'

'You took notes? What kind of notes?'

Oh, help... Mika had spotted the prices beside some of the dishes, like the *pesce del giorno*. Had they sent out their own boat to select the best fish the Mediterranean had to offer?

'Um, oh, interesting things. Like, there's a bit of confusion over whether that's a monastery or a convent. The church, *Santa Maria a Castro*, was there first. It was donated to the Dominican Friars in 1599 and they were the ones who built the convent. And…um…' She turned a page in the menu, distracted by the rumbling in her stomach. 'What are you going to have to eat?'

'Do you like pizza?'

'Of course.' Mika bit her lip. Did he really want to eat street food when there was so much more on offer? Or was he choosing the least expensive option because she had revealed too much when she'd said she'd waited a long time to get her flash camera? Had he guessed that she'd had to put so much effort into saving up for it? She could feel herself prickling defensively. She didn't need looking after financially. She didn't need looking after at all, in fact. Today had been an anomaly and it wasn't going to happen again.

'It goes with beer,' Rafe said smoothly. 'And they're usually so big I don't think I could eat one on my own.' He shrugged. 'I just thought that maybe we could share. How about this one? It's got wild mushrooms, asparagus, caramelised onion and *scamorza*. Do you know what *scamorza* is?'

'It's a cheese. Similar to mozzarella,'

'Sounds delicious.'

It did. And suddenly it was what Mika wanted to eat more than anything else on the menu. That the shared meal would be so affordable was merely a bonus.

Were they being watched by the staff? That might explain why—despite other tables being occupied—Rafe only had to glance up to have the waiter coming to take their order. But Mika couldn't help the feeling that this man was used to having control of his life. That he was one of that golden breed of people for whom things happened easily.

He had a problem now, though, didn't he?

He'd lost everything, she reminded herself.

And it was *her* fault.

Raoul could feel himself relaxing.

There'd been a moment when he'd thought the game was up because the *maître d'* had recognised him when he'd followed Mika into this small restaurant, but it seemed that it had simply been deference to his being Mika's male companion—an outdated assumption that he was in charge?

Whatever. It wasn't lost on Raoul that being in Mika's company, with people assuming they were a couple, was actually a layer of going incognito that he could never achieve on his own. Not that he would ever use someone like that, but it was an unexpected bonus. Like her company. Not only was she so easy to talk to, but every new snippet he was learning about her was adding to an impression that he was with a rather extraordinary person.

He didn't even have to say anything to communicate with her. Just a glance from those dark eyes, that seemed too big for the small face that framed them, had been enough to answer his concern that she might not want to sit beside a window that looked out over the kind of drop that had triggered her vertigo. The deliberate nudge of her foot had rewarded him with another glance and that one had cemented a bond. They were the only people in the world who knew about Mika's unfortunate experience up on that mountain track and it was going to stay that way. As far as anyone else was concerned, the journey would be memorable for ever because of the extraordinary view or the accomplishment of a not inconsiderable physical challenge.

How often did you find somebody that you could communicate with like that?

He'd seen it—between people like his grandparents, for instance—but they'd been together for decades and adored each other.

He and Mika were complete strangers.

Although, that strangeness was wearing off with every passing minute as he got to know more about her.

He'd glimpsed a dream by the way she handled that camera and a note in her voice when she'd told him that owning it had been a long time coming. Was she planning a new career as a photographer, perhaps? He already knew how determined she was by the way she'd handled her desperation at being in the clutches of vertigo, so he was quite confident that she would find a way to achieve any dreams she had.

Weirdly, it made him feel proud of her...

He'd also seen her pride. He'd deliberately searched for the least expensive item on the menu because it was obvious that Mika didn't have unlimited funds. He'd picked up on that, when she'd said she had waited a long time to own that precious camera, as easily as he'd been able to absorb communication from a glance. And he'd seen the way she'd reacted. It had reminded him of that curious little creature he'd come across for the first time when he'd been at his English boarding school—a hedgehog that curled itself into a ball to protect itself so that all you could see were prickles.

But Mika had relaxed again now. And she could *eat*… There was real pleasure to be found in the company of a female who actually tackled food like a boy. There was no picking at a low-calorie salad for Mika. She was attacking her big slices of pizza with so much enthusiasm, she had a big streak of tomato sauce on one cheek.

This was so different from anything he'd ever experienced. The only note of familiarity was the offer of the best table the restaurant had to offer—and another table would have been found, of course, for the discreet security personnel who were never far away. Photographers would have been shut outside for the moment but his female companion would have excused herself possibly more than once, to make sure she was ready for them later, to touch up her make-up and check that there were no stains on the figure-hugging evening gown she was wearing.

Imagining any of those elegant women he'd
dined with in the past with food on her face
made it virtually impossible to hide a smile.
Raoul also had to resist the urge to reach out
and wipe it clean with his napkin. Or maybe
just his thumb. He could imagine how the prickles would appear again if he did, though. He
already knew Mika quite well enough to know
that she would not appreciate being treated like
a child.

'It's good, isn't it?'

'So good.' Mika eyed the remaining slices
of the pizza but reached for her beer first. She
frowned at Raoul when she put her glass down.
'What's funny?'

The smile had escaped. 'You've got a mous-
tache.'

'Oh…' With the back of her hand, Mika
erased the foam above her lip. The gesture
captured the streak of tomato sauce as well.
'Better?'

'Mmm.' But Raoul was still smiling. He'd
never sat a table with a woman who would use
her hand rather than a napkin and it was quite
possible he'd never enjoyed a meal quite this
much, either.

'Tell me more about this OE you're on… Do you have an itinerary?'

'Not really. I find a place and a job and work until I've saved enough to go somewhere else. I'll be here for a while longer after investing in that camera, but it's a good job and I love it here, so that's okay.'

'What's your job?'

'I'm in hospo.'

Raoul blinked. Maybe his English wasn't as good as he'd thought. It took only as long as that blink for Mika to realise his lack of comprehension and rescue him.

'Hospitality. I'm a waitress in a café down in Positano.'

'And that's a good job?'

'It is when you're travelling. It's easy to get work and nobody's too bothered about permits or anything. You can get paid in cash, too. It's what most people do on their OE. Part of the rite of passage, even. Everybody should work in hospo at least once.'

'Why?'

'Because it changes the way you see the world. You get to see the best and worst of people in ways you wouldn't believe. And it changes how you see people who work in the kind of jobs that usually make them invisible—you know what I mean?'

Raoul nodded slowly but his interest had been piqued. How many people were there in his world that quietly came and went, making life easier for himself and his family? Advisors and bodyguards. Cooks and cleaners. He'd never served anyone so he had no idea what life would look like from that kind of perspective. He was ashamed to realise he hadn't even given it much thought.

Until now…

So that kind of job could change the way you saw the world… Was that what *he* needed to do?

There was only one slice of pizza left.

'You have it,' Raoul said.

'No, it's all yours. You're a boy. You need to eat more.'

'How about we go halves?'

Mika's face lit up. 'Okay.' She tore the big triangle into two pieces and then eyed them up.

'That one is bigger,' Raoul pointed out. 'You have it.'

Mika hesitated for a moment then she picked up the larger piece and took a big bite out of it before putting it down again.

Raoul snorted with laughter. 'Okay, now they're the same. I choose this one.' He picked up the piece that now had a semicircle of tooth marks where the point of the triangle had been, his hand grazing hers as it passed. Or maybe it hadn't actually touched her skin—it just felt like it had—because she didn't move hers further away. His gaze met Mika's over the slice as he bit into it…and there it was again…

That feeling of a connection he'd never felt before.

Was this what having a real friend was like?

Oddly, it was as exciting as that first flutter of physical attraction could be.

Mika washed down the last of her pizza with the last swallow of her beer. She sighed with contentment and then leaned back in her chair.

'Right, mister. What are we going to do with you?'

The expression on her face was a mix of concern and a determination to fix things. She was fiddling with the charm on her necklace in a way that suggested it was an automatic accompaniment to a process of deep thought.

The irony wasn't lost on Raoul.

'Why do you wear a dolphin charm?'

Mika's fingers stilled. She was staring at him

with those huge eyes and Raoul felt that he'd stepped over a boundary of some kind. He'd asked a question that had personal significance and, right now, she was weighing up whether or not to trust him with an honest response.

'It's a symbol,' she finally said softly. 'Of being wild and free. And…and happy.'

The wistful note in her voice went straight to Raoul's heart and struck a very unexpected chord.

Mika was searching for happiness, as everybody did, but she was already almost as wild and free as one of the beautiful creatures his homeland had been named for. She didn't have to step into a life that was pretty much set in stone—a life that meant personal happiness was unimportant compared to the greater good. If happiness was there, as it had been for most of his life, it was a bonus.

Raoul envied her. Okay, there was a twinge of sympathy that she hadn't yet found her ultimate happiness, but she was free to create it. To go anywhere and do anything that might help her reach her goal.

As if she knew she might have revealed too much, Mika lifted her hand away from the charm and pushed her fingers through her already spiky hair.

'What are you going to do?' she asked bluntly. 'I can't go home and leave you out on the streets. Not when it's my fault you're in this predicament.'

'What would you do, if you were me?'

She probably didn't notice that her fingers strayed back to the dolphin charm. 'I guess I'd find somewhere to stay and then I'd find a job. If you can get one like mine, you get at least one meal a day thrown in as well. It all helps.'

Raoul nodded. Something was falling into place in his head. Impressions and ideas that had been accumulating over the course of this dinner. He'd set out on this private journey to learn about himself but what if he was approaching his quest from the wrong angle? What if he actually needed to learn about *other* people? The invisible kind, like those in service? Or the individuals amongst a mass like the people he would very soon be ruling?

He could get himself out of his predicament with a simple phone call.

Or, he could embrace his situation by deciding that fate had provided an opportunity that would have been unthinkable even a few hours ago. He could see if he had the personal fortitude to face being homeless. Penniless and without even the prospect of a job. How many of his own people had faced a challenge like this at some time in their lives?

He'd been silent for so long that Mika was chewing her lip and frowning, as if she was trying to solve the problem of world peace rather than his own immediate future.

'Have you ever worked in hospo?'

He shook his head. 'Never.'

'Oh…it's just that our café is really busy with the start of the high season. I reckon you could get a job there too.'

'I could try.'

'You wouldn't cope if you've never done it before. With no experience, probably the only job you'd get would be washing dishes.' Her eyes widened. 'The dishie we've got was talking about moving on yesterday. I'll bet Marco hasn't found a replacement yet.'

Washing dishes. Had he *ever* had to wash dishes? Meals away from his residential apartment at university had always been in restaurants, like meals away from the mess during his time with the military. As for the palace…

he hadn't even been near the kitchens since he'd been a small child in search of an extra treat.

Dishwashing was possibly one of the most ordinary jobs there was out here in the real world. And wasn't 'ordinary' exactly what he'd set out to be in this time away from his real world?

'I… I wouldn't mind washing dishes.'

Mika's nod was solemn. It was her turn to be silent for a while now. At last she spoke, and he could see by the way her throat moved as she swallowed first that she was making a huge effort.

'I owe you one, Rafe…for today. There's a couch in my room that you can sleep on tonight…as long as…'

She wouldn't meet his gaze. There was something important that she didn't want to say. Something about her body language reminded him of the hedgehog again. She was poised to curl into a ball to protect herself. With a flash, he realised what it could be and the thought was horrific. Had she been hurt by a man? Did that explain the way she'd reacted when he'd touched her? How hesitant she'd been to take his hand even when she'd been desperate?

'Mika…' He waited until she looked up and,

yes, he could see uncertainty. It wasn't fear, exactly, because there was a fierceness that told him she was well practised in defending herself. But she was clearly offering him something that was well out of her comfort zone.

He resisted the urge to touch her hand. Eye contact was more than enough, and even that he kept as gentle as he could. 'We're friends now, yes?'

Mika nodded but she wasn't quite meeting his gaze.

'You're safe with me. I give you my word.'

She looked straight at him, then, and for a heartbeat, and then another, she held his gaze, as if she was searching for confirmation that his word was trustworthy.

That she found what she was looking for was revealed by no more than a softening of her face but Raoul could feel the gift of her trust as if it was solid enough to hold in his hands.

His vow was equally silent.

He would not drop that gift and break it.

CHAPTER THREE

WHO KNEW THAT military training would end up being so useful in the daily life of an ordinary person?

It meant that Raoul de Poitier was conditioned well enough that yesterday's strenuous exercise had been no more than a good workout. It also meant that he'd been able to sleep on a lumpy old couch that was actually a lot more comfortable than sleeping on the ground.

He'd tapped into a bit of initiative in making the best use of available resources, too. Mika had a laptop computer and he'd borrowed it for long enough to send an email to his grandmother to let her know he was safe but not to expect to hear from him for a little while.

Mika had been busy with her technology for a while after that, downloading photographs she had taken that day, her busy tapping suggesting she was adding notes to the images.

Her frequent glances away from the screen told him that she wasn't entirely comfortable having him share this small space; the idea to turn the couch around so that the back of it faced into the small room came to him in a flash of inspiration. The effect of the change had been to create the illusion of a wall and, once he was lying down—with his legs bent and his knees propped on the wall—he couldn't see Mika in the single bed that was only a few feet away. Any tension ebbed as it became apparent that the arrangement would give her more privacy as she worked and then slept.

The bathroom facilities were shared with all the other occupants of the rooms on that floor of the old boarding house. That had been more of a shock than Raoul had expected after a lifetime of a sparkling clean, private *en suite* bathroom always having been available but, on the plus side, there was no queue at this early hour of the morning.

Mika wasn't due to start her shift in the café until eight a.m. but it opened at six a.m. and she was taking him in to meet the owner, Marco, in the hope that there might be some work available for a new dish-washer. She'd used the bathroom first and came out in her uniform of a short black skirt and a fitted short-sleeved black shirt. It was an outfit designed to cloak a member of the army of invisible people and, when Mika tied on a pretty white apron with a frill around its edge, he realised the uniform was probably also intended to make her look demure.

The shirt certainly covered the tattoo on her arm but Raoul doubted that anything would make Mika look demure—not with that aura of feistiness, combined with the impression of intelligence that one glance at her face was enough to discern.

'It's a horrible job,' she warned Raoul. 'A dishie has to be a food-hand as well and help with the food prep to start the day, with jobs like chopping onions and making sauce, and then he has to keep up with all the dishes as soon as service starts, and that's not easy.'

'I'm sure I could get up to speed.' How hard could it be to do such menial work? This was the twenty-first century. Even a small establishment would have commercial dishwashing machines, surely?

Mika turned a corner as they headed downhill towards the beach. They walked past a series of shops still shuttered and sleeping in the soft light of a new day.

'Dishies get yelled at by the chefs if they get behind,' Mika continued. 'The waitresses hate finding they've suddenly run out of cutlery or something and the *barista* will have a tantrum if he runs out of coffee cups.'

'Who's in charge?'

Mika looked up to grin at him. 'Marco *thinks* he is but everybody has to keep the head chef happy. A dishie is right at the bottom of the pecking order, though. He has to keep *everybody* happy.'

Raoul wondered where the waitresses fitted into the pecking order. He would do his best to keep Mika happy if he got this job.

It was a surprise to realise how much he *wanted* to get this job. It wasn't simply the opportunity of gaining a different perspective on life—the idea of it was beginning to tap into a yearning that went way back.

Didn't every kid dream of being invisible at some time? And maybe that fantasy had more meaning to those who grew up under a very public spotlight. He would be visible to the people he worked with here, of course, but it felt like he would be stepping into an alternative reality. Nobody who knew him would expect to see him in this kind of work and that would be enough to make him blend into the background, even if they took notice of the people who spent their lives in service of some kind.

'Here it is.' Mika began to cross the cobbled street to a shop front that had canvas awnings over the footpath. The name of the café was printed on the dark terracotta canvas in big, white, cursive letters—*Pane Quotidiano*—the 'Daily Bread'.

A short, middle-aged man with a long, white apron tied around an ample waist was lifting wrought-iron chairs from a stack to position around small tables. '*Buongiorno*, Marco.'

'*Buongiorno,* Mika. Why are you so early?'

'I've brought a friend—Rafe. He needs a job. Is Pierre still here?'

Marco threw his hands in the air and his huff of breath was exasperated. 'He walked out yesterday, would you believe? Demanded his money and that was that.' Raoul was receiving a shrewd glance. 'You got any experience?'

'I learn fast,' Raoul replied in Italian—the language Mika was speaking with impressive fluency. 'Try me.'

Marco had his hands on his hips now as he assessed Raoul.

'He speaks English,' Mika put in.

'And French,' Raoul added. And Dauphin-esque, but that was hardly likely to be useful to the majority of tourists this café served, and he had no intention of giving anybody such a clue to his nationality.

'Makes no difference.' Marco shrugged. 'All he needs to know is how to follow orders and work hard.'

'Try me,' Raoul said again. He should prob-ably have added 'please' but, curiously, it ran-kled that he was being assessed and possibly found wanting. Not something he was used to, that was for sure.

'One day,' Marco said grudgingly. 'You do a good job, I will hire you. Mess up and you won't get paid for today.'

A glance at Mika gave him another one of those lightning-fast, telepathic messages. This was a good deal and, if he wanted the job, he'd better grab the opportunity.

Marco was clearly confident he had an extra set of hands for the day, at least.

'Finish putting these chairs out,' he told Raoul. 'And then come back into the kitchen. Mika? Seeing as you're here so early, make me a coffee.'

'One macchiato coming right up.' Mika

didn't seem bothered by the crisp order. She was looking delighted, in fact, by the way this job interview had panned out. She gave Raoul a quick thumbs-up sign as she disappeared into the café behind her boss.

His boss, too, if he could prove himself today. Raoul lifted a couple of the heavy chairs and carried them to the table on the far side of the outdoor area. As he went back for more, he caught sight of himself in the windows that hadn't yet been folded back to open up the café to catch the breeze and what he saw made him catch his breath and look again.

He'd had to comb his hair with his fingers this morning so it was more tousled than he'd ever seen before. He'd rinsed out his only set of clothes and hung them over the tiny line outside the window of Mika's room, so they were clean enough, but so wrinkled it looked as if he'd slept in them for a week. He'd noticed that the stubble on his jaw had felt a lot smoother yesterday but now he could see that it was beginning to look like a proper beard.

Nobody was going to recognise him. He barely recognised himself.

He wasn't a prince here. Nobody had even asked him for a surname. He was just an ordinary guy called Rafe. And Rafe was on the way to finding his first paid employment.

Maybe he was delighted as well.

The trickle of breakfast customers had grown into a steady stream of holiday makers who preferred a relaxed brunch. Mika's section today covered all the street tables so she had the added hazard of stepping around dogs lying by their owners' chairs as she delivered plates of hot food or trays laden with coffee orders. Tables were being taken as soon as people stood up to leave so they had to be wiped down fast, and a new carafe of chilled water along with glasses provided.

She was almost too busy to wonder how Rafe was coping out the back but he entered her thoughts every time she cleared a table, being careful to scrape the plates and put all the cutlery on the top. Carrying the piles to the kitchen, she found herself scanning shelves to see where they were running low on supplies.

'We're going to need more water glasses soon. And don't forget the lemon slices and sprigs of mint in the carafes.'

'Okay.' Rafe had a huge apron on and a dish brush in his hand. He started to push a pile of plates further towards the sinks so that Mika had room to put hers down.

'Careful…' Without thinking, Mika caught his hand. 'Margaret's left cutlery between the plates. That whole pile could topple and smash on the floor.' She could feel the heat of his skin beneath her fingers. Had it been soaking in hot water for too long to feel as if it was burning her? Hastily, she pulled her hand away and scooped up the knives and forks on her top plate to put them into the big, sudsy bucket on the floor. Pierre, the last dish-washer, had trained her not to drop them too fast and splash his legs.

'Thanks.' Rafe cast an eye over his shoulder and lowered his voice. 'I don't want to annoy him again. He had to show me how to run the dishwasher twice.'

Mika smiled. 'Gianni's bark is worse than his bite. He's a pretty good chef.'

'*Service*… Table eight.'

'Oh, that's me…' Mika turned swiftly, uncomfortably aware that she'd been distracted. 'Behind,' she called in warning on her way to the pass, as one of the other waitresses backed through the swing door with another tray of dirty dishes. Would she have room to dump them on the bench? Rafe was going to have to work faster if he wanted to get this job. He might not even get a break, at the rate he was going.

There were plenty of water glasses on the shelf the next time she settled new customers and every carafe was decorated with mint and lemon. This was good. Rafe hadn't been exaggerating when he'd promised Marco that he was a fast learner. Mika delivered another tray of coffees to the table where her boss was sitting—as usual—with a couple of his mates, right on the footpath, so he could greet anyone else he knew and keep an eye on how the whole café was functioning. If things got really crazy, he would pitch in to help, or sometimes he would just wander around to check that everybody was enjoying their time in Positano's best café. He had the best job, which was fair enough, given that he was the owner of the establishment.

Poor Rafe had the worst job but he seemed to be managing. Mika stopped worrying about him as the day sped on. It wasn't her problem if he didn't like the work or didn't get offered a paid job, was it? She'd repaid her debt by giving him dinner and a place to stay last night. Finding him work was just a bonus.

Except…

She liked him. And she liked having him around. Instead of grumpy Pierre, whom she had to be careful not to splash, she could look forward to a smile every time she carried dirty dishes out the back.

It was growing on her, that smile.

The other waitresses must be getting smiled at too, she decided. There was a faint undercurrent of something different amongst her colleagues today. They seemed to be putting more effort into being charming with the customers. Was it her imagination or was Margaret, the English girl who was here to improve her Italian, making more frequent trips to the kitchen than usual? She'd spotted Bianca reapplying her lipstick more than once and Alain, the gay barista, had even gone to collect clean coffee cups himself instead of calling for one of the waitresses to do it.

No surprises there. Hospitality workers were usually young, travelling and eager for any fun that came their way. Rafe was new.

And gorgeous…

It was his eyes even more than that smile.

The warmth in them. And that wicked gleam of humour. Would she ever forget the way he'd looked at her over that slice of pizza that she'd already taken the huge bite out of? It had been a silly joke but he'd bought right into it and for a heartbeat, as she'd been caught in his gaze, she'd felt like she'd known him for ever.

Like he was her best friend. Or the brother she'd never had.

'Sorry?' Mika had to scrabble to retrieve her pad from the pocket of her apron. She pulled her pencil from behind her ear. 'Was that one seafood risotto?'

'Two.' The customer glared at her. 'And the linguine with lobster. And side salads. And we need some more water.'

'No problem. Coming right up.'

Mika stepped over a sleeping poodle, dodged a small child and turned sideways to give Margaret room to carry a tray past her.

'Thanks, hon.'

Margaret had a nice smile, too. And long blonde hair. And legs that went on for ever under that short skirt.

Mika ducked into the kitchen to put the order for table six under the rail above the grill. She glanced sideways to see Rafe scraping plates into the rubbish bucket. He had promised that she was safe with him and he certainly hadn't done anything to undermine that promise last night. They were friends. He hadn't given her so much as a glance that might have suggested any kind of attraction and that was exactly what she'd wanted.

So what if he was tempted to hook up with Margaret? Or Bianca? Or even Alain for that matter? It was none of her business and she wasn't bothered.

With a sigh, Mika collected another carafe of water and headed back to table six.

It wasn't completely true, was it?

She *was* bothered.

It was that smile that was doing it. Other people smiled at her and it could make her feel good but there was something about Rafe's smile that made her feel much better than good. It felt like her body was waking up after a long, long sleep and that every cell was tingling in the bright light of a brand new day. She was over-sensitive to the slightest touch, like the way his hand had barely brushed hers in taking that piece of pizza last night. Or the heat of his hand when she'd laid her fingers over the back of it to stop him unbalancing that pile of crockery.

The tingling bordered on being painful. And it was confusing. She didn't *want* to feel this way but there it was. Like that horrible vertigo, it had just appeared from nowhere.

And, now that it was here, she didn't really want it to go away, either. It was making her feel so…alive…

Forty euros.

Raoul stared at the notes in his hand. For more than ten hours of back-breakingly hard work, it was a pittance but, having had no more than enough for a bus fare in his pockets at the start of the day, it looked like a small fortune.

It was a clever ploy of Marco's to give him cash at the end of his day's trial as well as offering him as many shifts as he wanted to take in the café. If he hadn't had actual money in his hand right now, it would be very tempting not to show up tomorrow.

Military training hadn't set him up very well for this particular challenge. His hands felt waterlogged and swollen and he had tiny cuts from not handling the cutlery well enough that would probably sting later. His back ached from so many hours standing and, even though he'd wolfed down a meal when he'd finally been given a break, he was starving again already.

'You did it.' Mika was waiting for him outside the café and her expression made him think of a proud mother collecting her child from their first day at school. 'Go you.'

Suddenly Raoul felt proud of himself, too. 'It was a close call. When I forgot to warn Gianna that I was behind him and he dropped a whole pizza, I thought I was going to get fired on the spot.'

Mika shrugged. 'Worse things happen. Pierre had a huge stack of dishes crash onto the floor and smash when he started.'

'Did he have to pay for them?'

She shook her head. 'If Marco had expected that, he would have lost his worker as well as the dishes. People working in hospo don't usually have that kind of money and employers can't afford to chase them.'

'Why not?'

'It's easy employment. Casual. If we get paid in cash, we don't have to worry about paying tax, and employers can get away with paying less than minimum rates. It works for everyone.'

Raoul was frowning as he walked alongside Mika. Taxes were essential because they paid for things like hospitals and schools but he could understand why having part of an already low wage removed would add insult to injury. What was the minimum acceptable rate to pay people in his own country? And how much tax were they expected to pay?

He should know things like this.

'What's wrong?'

'Nothing…why did you ask?'

'You sighed. It sounded like you had the weight of the whole world on your shoulders.'

'Oh…' He'd have to be a bit careful what he thought about while he was with Mika. 'I'm a bit tired, I guess. It's been quite a long day.'

'I know how to fix that.'

'Oh?' The sound was wary. Considering that Mika had been racing around working just as hard as he had been for the same length of time, she looked remarkably chirpy. Raoul hoped she wasn't going to suggest an evening in a nightclub when he knew that all he would want to do later would be to sleep.

And he might need to find a place to sleep. Mika had only offered him a night on her couch.

'Do your feet hurt? Is your back sore? Have you got a bit of a headache?'

'Ah…yes, yes and yes.'

Raoul was beginning to wonder how long he might have the fortitude to keep it up, in fact. He'd never spent such a concentrated length of time doing such menial tasks. How horrified would his grandmother be if she knew? How astonished would his people be if they found out? In public opinion, it would be beneath his station in life—the work of servants.

But what made *him* so special, other than an accident of birth? Equality was a core value of the constitution of his land. Other people did this kind of work and some did it for their entire working lives. And Mika had worked just as hard today, hadn't she?

She was nodding, as if agreeing with his unspoken thoughts. 'Me too. And I know the cure.'

'Wine?' Raoul suggested hopefully. 'Sleep?'

Mika laughed. 'A swim. It's what I usually do when I have time after work. I collect my bathing suit and jump on a bus to Praiano and go down to my favourite beach. Want to come with me?'

'I don't have a bathing suit.'

'You could just wear your shorts. It would save washing them later.' Mika's head turned, scanning the tourist shops they were passing that were still open. 'You should get another tee shirt, though. Let's have a look.'

Raoul had to stop as well but he shook his head. 'I can't afford a tee shirt. It's my turn to buy dinner tonight and…and I need to find somewhere to stay. I'll need money for that, too.'

'But you've got somewhere to stay.' Mika seemed to have gone very still, her hand touching the rack of tee shirts on the footpath. 'If you don't mind the couch.'

Raoul blinked. 'You want me to stay?'

'I know it's not ideal but it's only for sleeping, and you're only here for a few weeks. I'm either at work or out exploring for the rest of the time. I'm happy to share if you are.'

She was making it sound as if it was fine if he liked the idea but she wouldn't be at all bothered if he decided otherwise. Her attention seemed to be on the shirts as she began to ruffle through them. Her tone and body language didn't quite fit with the flash of something he'd seen in her eyes, though. It wasn't any kind of come-on—she'd made it quite clear she wasn't interested in anything more than friendship—but there was something that made him think she would like him to agree to the plan a lot more than she was letting on.

Was Mika *lonely*…?

Part of him was more than a bit horrified by the idea of continuing to live in one room and share a bathroom with who knew how many other people, but was it because he was spoiled and soft or was it more to do with always having to be over-vigilant as to what others might think? When you lived in the public eye you had to behave perfectly at all times because you never knew if you were under observation by a journalist or the paparazzi. For as long as he could remember, he'd never been able to be impulsive and just do what he happened to feel like doing. Or even let how he was feeling show on his face sometimes.

But now he could. Nobody was watching. If his reluctance stemmed from the fact he was spoiled, it would do him good to toughen up. And if it was because of what others might think, well, there were no rules he had to follow other than his personal morality right now. What would happen if he really let his guard down?

'Maybe one more night? We can talk about it again tomorrow. Right now, I love your idea of a swim.'

Mika nodded. 'Stay here. Buy a tee shirt and maybe some shorts to swim in. Look, this might help...' She put her hand in her pocket and when it came out she was holding a small handful of gold-rimmed silver coins. 'I always put all my tips in the communal jar but...' Her shrug made light of any residual guilt. 'I thought we might have something to celebrate tonight.'

'No way.' Raoul put his hand over Mika's to close her fingers firmly around the coins. Such a small hand. He liked the way his could enclose it completely. 'You earned that. You keep it.' His voice was stern. 'You've got to stop paying for things for me, okay? I'm beginning to feel like a gigolo.'

Mika was smiling as she pulled her hand free and put the coins back in her pocket, but she avoided meeting his gaze, and Raoul gave himself a mental shake. Gigolos were rewarded for services that he had no intention of offering, and that would be the last thing Mika wanted anyway.

'I'll be back in ten minutes.' Mika was already walking away from him and it felt like a rebuke. Perhaps even a subtle reference to sex was dodgy territory that he needed to steer well clear of. 'Happy shopping.'

* * *

A gigolo?

With those looks and that charm, there would probably be any number of rich older woman who would be happy to have Rafe at their beck and call. While Mika knew that the comment had been no more than a joke, it had sexual connotations that had put her well out of her comfort zone.

Had she turned into some kind of prude in the last few years?

Or was it because it was Rafe who had said it and that was tapping into feelings she wasn't sure how to deal with yet?

And why had she been so quick to renew the offer of having him sleep on her couch? Did she want that painful prickle of awareness to get worse? Was she trying to test herself in some way?

Maybe she was but it wasn't something she wanted to think about because, if she did, she'd find somewhere to hide. She could find the concierge of this boarding house, perhaps, and see if there was an empty room that Rafe could rent.

Tomorrow would be soon enough for that. Right now, she needed to hurry, to change out of her uniform and put her bikini on under her favourite shorts and singlet top. She swapped her soft, black tennis shoes for lightweight sandals and draped her towel over her arm. With her camera hanging from her shoulder, she was ready to go and find Rafe.

She'd made this trip for a swim after work many times already but how much better was it to have company?

Company that was now wearing a huge white tee shirt with *I heart Positano* emblazoned on the front. Rafe didn't look the least bit embarrassed to be wearing it.

'It was on the sale rack,' he told her. 'An absolute bargain.'

'Mmm…' Mika's lips twitched. 'Fair enough. I heart Positano, too. Oh…there's our bus down the road. We'll have to run.'

The bus was crowded and they had to stand but the journey was short enough for it not to matter. Mika led him down the cobbled alleyways in the heart of Praiano and many steps that led down to a beach that had no sand. There were rows of sun loungers to hire, like on every European beach, but they were on a huge, flagged terrace, and further back there were tables and chairs spilling out from a beachside café. Rock music was also spilling out and the place was crowded with young people.

Mika made a beeline for a couple of empty loungers and she put her camera on one and covered it with her towel. Then she kicked off her sandals and peeled her singlet top off. Taking her shorts off in front of Rafe gave her an odd feeling, as though something had thumped her painlessly in her belly. A sideways glance showed that he wasn't taking any notice, however. He was too busy pulling off his new tee shirt. The sight of all that bare skin created ripples from the thumping sensation that felt like small electric shocks. It sent Mika swiftly to the edge of the terrace where she could dive straight into the deep, cool water.

The sea had always been her ultimate comfort zone. It was her place of choice to unwind and to think clearly, and it was definitely the best place to burn off angst of any kind, whether it was emotional, physical or—like now—possibly a combination of both.

She knew Rafe had dived in right behind her but Mika wasn't here to float around or play, like most of the other young couples in the water. She set out for the pontoon that was moored a hundred metres or so offshore. And when she became aware that Rafe was keeping pace, she doubled her efforts. This was a race she knew she could win.

'Where did you learn to swim like that?'

The words were hard to get out because Raoul was unexpectedly out-of-breath by the time he heaved himself up onto the pontoon. Mika was already sitting on the edge, her feet just touching the water.

'My mother always said I had dolphin blood.' Mika didn't seem at all out of breath. 'I grew up by the sea and apparently I could swim even before I could walk properly.'

Raoul smiled, liking that idea. Yes…there was something about Mika that reminded him of the creatures his homeland was named for. Confident and a little bit cheeky. Graceful… He'd seen Mika moving around the café today, twisting and turning her body to ease through small spaces or avoid obstacles. Friendly but still wild. Yes, you could touch them sometimes, but it was an honour to be allowed to do so.

They were both sitting on the edge of the pontoon, facing the shore, where they could see the crowd in the popular bar growing. They could still hear the music from here and it was a quieter number—a folk song that was wistful enough almost to create a sensation of yearning…

A need to feel less alone by connecting with another human being…

'I don't remember my mother very well,' Raoul said quietly. 'She died, along with my father, in a plane crash when I was only five.'

People were always shocked that he'd been orphaned so early but the glance Mika gave him had no pity in it.

'I wish I'd never known mine very well,' she said. 'Maybe it wouldn't have hurt so much when she abandoned me.'

Raoul was definitely shocked. '*Abandoned* you? How?'

'She took me into the city for the day. Put me in the play area of a big department store and just never came back.'

'How old were you?'

'I was five, too. I'd just started school.'

Wow… To have lost a parent at such a vulnerable age was something that he'd never found he had in common with anyone. Ever. Even now, he could remember how lost he'd felt. How empty his world had suddenly become.

Had Mika had loving grandparents to fill

such an appalling void? A small army of kind nannies, tutors and so many others, like cooks and gardeners, who would go out of their way every day to make a small, orphaned prince feel special?

'What happened? Who looked after you?'

'The police were called. I got put in the hands of the social welfare people and they found a foster home.'

'Did the police find your mother?'

'Oh…eventually. She turned up dead about ten years later. Drug overdose. Maybe she thought she was doing me a favour by shutting me out of her life.'

'What about your father?'

'Don't have one. My mother never told me anything about him other than that he was Scottish. A backpacker she'd met in a bar somewhere. I have no way of tracing him. No idea of where I came from, really.'

'I'm sorry…'

'Don't be. It has a good side. I'm as free as a bird. Or a dolphin, maybe. I can't imagine living away from the sea. I had to do that in a couple of foster homes and I hated the cities.'

Raoul was silent for a long moment. He could trace his family back to the twelfth century when their islands had become a principality. He knew every drop of his bloodline and almost every square mile of the place that was where he came from and where he would always belong.

How lost would someone feel not to have that kind of foundation? Did he really envy the freedom she'd had in comparison to how precisely his own life was mapped out?

Was that what Mika was looking for—a place where she felt she belonged? A life that offered the safety of a real home? How much heartache had been covered by that casual reference to 'a couple of foster homes'? How often had she been passed from home to home? Abandoned again and again?

The sun was low now and Mika's nut-brown skin seemed to have taken on a golden glow as Raoul's silent questions led him to turn his head towards her. Her bikini was white—small scraps of fabric that left very little to the imagination.

It wasn't his imagination that was his undoing, though.

Mika had her hands shading her eyes from the glare of the setting sun so she didn't see him looking at her. She might be tiny, Raoul decided, but she was most definitely perfectly formed. And *real*... It would probably never occur to Mika to make her breasts larger or wear killer heels to make herself look taller and sexier. He couldn't imagine her plastering her face with make-up, either. She didn't need it, with those amazing eyes of hers.

She was...gorgeous.

He'd come to the conclusion that Mika was an extraordinary person within a short time of knowing her and learning about her rough start in life somehow didn't surprise him.

What did surprise him—and not in a good way—was the strength of the attraction he was feeling towards her right now. Had either of them really been aware of how close to each other they were sitting? He would only have to relax his arm a little for their shoulders to touch. He could feel the warmth of her skin just thinking about it.

His hands tightened on the edge of the pontoon as he realised how much he *wanted* to touch Mika. He pressed his lips together to try and stifle the urge to kiss her.

Given the uncanny way they could communicate with no more than a glance, it was unfortunate that Mika chose that moment to lower her hands and turn her head.

For too long, she held his gaze. Too long, because Raoul knew that she was aware of him physically, too. That the attraction might well be mutual.

It couldn't happen. Not when, in a matter of a few short weeks, he had to step back into his real life and prepare to marry the woman he'd been promised to for almost as long as he could remember. The engagement was about to become official, which had to put an end to any sexual adventures, and surely he'd had enough over the years, anyway?

He'd never known anybody like Mika, though, had he?

Maybe being homeless and poor wasn't going to be the ultimate challenge that would tell him whether he could be the ruler his people deserved. Perhaps *this* was going to be the biggest test. Could he put aside his personal desires in order to do what he knew was the right thing to do?

It would be shameful if he couldn't.

The tumble of his thoughts took no longer than the shared glance. It was Mika who broke the eye contact, and she did it so abruptly, Raoul was left wondering if he'd imagined what he thought he'd seen. Or had she been shocked by what *she'd* seen?

'Hot chips,' she said.

'What?' The randomness of the words cleared his mind with a jolt.

'Bernie—the guy who runs the bar on the beach. He's English and I think he was in a band that did quite well back in the seventies. He makes the best hot chips I've ever tasted. Everyone comes here for his fish and chips, and I've just realised that I'm absolutely *starving.*' Her grin held all the cheek he was coming to expect from Mika. 'I seem to remember you saying something about it being your turn to buy dinner?'

'I did. And it is.'

'Race you back, then…'

It was a huge relief to sink into the chill of the seawater. As good as a cold shower, in fact.

He could do this, Raoul decided. He could enjoy the company of the first genuine friend he'd ever made without ruining that friendship with sex. That way, Mika wouldn't end up being hurt, and it could be possible that the friendship might never be completely lost. Sure, Mika would get a shock when she found out who he really was, but by then maybe she would know him well enough to understand and forgive the deception.

This feeling of connection to another person was too special to lose.

Raoul had a distinct feeling that he might never experience it again.

CHAPTER FOUR

HAD SHE IMAGINED IT?

That buzz of physical awareness she'd seen in Rafe's eyes when they'd been sitting side by side on the pontoon, in the glow of a sunset, the other night…

Maybe it had just been a product of a combination of things. The gorgeous sunset, how relaxed a swim in the sea could make you feel after a long, hard day at work, and the fact that they were both as close to naked as public decency allowed. If—for a moment in time—Rafe had fancied her, he had done nothing to confirm any interest since.

And Mika would have noticed the slightest indication because she'd been so nervous about it. Emotionally, she'd run as hard and fast as she could when she thought she'd seen it. She'd tried to wash away the confused jumble of feelings by swimming hard enough to beat Rafe back to the shore, and had kept the conversation deliberately impersonal as they'd eaten the fish and chips that Rafe had declared the best he'd ever tasted after she'd snapped a few photos of the fading sunset and their surroundings. One of Rafe, too, that he hadn't even seen her taking.

He'd been standing watching that sunset— one hand shading his eyes, the other holding the damp towel he had insisted she used first. His hair had been still wet and drops were landing on his shoulders to trickle onto that bare chest. There'd been something poignant in the way he was staring out to sea and even through the lens of her camera the beauty of this man had been enough to give Mika that curious sensation in her belly again—the thump and the electric tingles of physical attraction.

The action had been instinctive. Something had told her that there could well be a time she'd want to remember this day and this man who'd stirred these feelings she thought she'd lost for ever. It was an action that had taken only a split second and was as private as the reasons she had taken it.

It had been only a momentary blip in the impersonal atmosphere that Mika had been determined to foster as a safety buffer zone, and the tactic had worked so well that it had cemented what seemed to have become a pattern. They did their long shifts at the café, went for a swim after work, ate a meal that they took turns paying for and, by the time they got home after dark, they were both so tired that sleep was essential before another early rise.

Had the tactic worked *too* well?

A couple of days later, Mika realised that her nervousness had evaporated. That she had to conclude that she *had* imagined any desire on Rafe's part.

And, if she was really honest, there was a part of her that was...what?...disappointed?

Frustrated, even?

If things had been different—if *she* was different—that moment on the pontoon could have played out in a very different way.

She would have seen that look in Rafe's eyes and fallen into it instead of running away. They would have held that eye contact as they'd slowly closed the distance between them and then...then she would have felt Rafe's lips against her own...

The way she had so many times in those unguarded moments of the last few nights when she'd been slipping into sleep and could hear the sound of Rafe's breathing only a few feet away. The intensity of her body's reaction to the fantasy kiss had been enough to make her think that she'd never wanted anything as much as she wanted Rafe to kiss her.

But it wasn't going to happen, was it? Oh, he still seemed to be enjoying her company. He still smiled just as readily. But there was something different about the way he looked at her. Or *didn't* look at her. Yes, that was it. There was a wariness that hadn't been there before. That connection that she felt when her gaze met his was missing…because he never held her gaze long enough for it to kick in.

Because he was avoiding it?

Had he seen her fear?

Mika's thoughts seemed to be a series of questions that were becoming increasingly unsettling.

Would she react the same way if she had another chance?

Did she *want* another chance?

Part of her seemed to. Otherwise, she wouldn't have had a quiet word with Marco yesterday to ask if Rafe could have the same day off as she had this week. She wouldn't have told him about her plan to explore the valley of the ancient mills in Amalfi and slipped in that casual invitation for him to join her if he had nothing else he wanted to do with his day off.

They wouldn't be here now, standing in the central square of Amalfi beside the cathedral stairs, gazing at the narrow, cobbled streets and trying to decide which one would take them uphill to where they would find the entrance to the valley.

A woman walking a small dog glanced at Rafe and paused. Smiling, she asked if they needed any help.

'Please,' Rafe answered. 'We're looking for the way to the Valley of the Mills.'

'Ah…the *Valle dei Mulini*… Go up the main street here, which leads into *Via Pietro Capuano*…'

Mika was listening to the directions but she was also watching the body language in front of her. Did Rafe know the effect he had on women? Of course he did, she decided. How could he not know?

He could have anyone he chose, couldn't he?

Was it no more than a fantasy that he might choose *her*?

The answer to that was simple. Of course it was. He saw her as a friend, nothing more. And maybe this was the best thing that could have happened for her—the reason why fate had made him appear in her life. She could play with the possibility of something physical developing in her mind, and perhaps that was the step she needed to take so that she would be ready when someone came into her life that she was attracted to—someone who wanted to be with *her*.

Someone other than Rafe…

'Did you get all that?' The woman and her dog were walking away. Rafe's glance was unreadable.

'Yep. Let's go.' Oddly, the excitement of this adventure had faded a little for Mika.

'We go past the paper museum. You want to go there, don't you?'

'Mmm…' Mika was slightly ahead of Rafe now. 'It won't be open yet, though. I'll go on the way back. You don't have to do the museum, though, if they're not your thing.'

They walked in silence until they'd passed the museum and reached a set of steps going uphill. Rafe went ahead of Mika as they climbed the steps and, by the time they'd walked on for a few more minutes, the silence had become awkward.

'Can we stop for a second? I'd like to take a photo of that lemon grove.'

Rafe stopped. He turned and, for the first time in days, Mika found her gaze properly caught.

'Would you rather be doing this by yourself?'

'What? No…of course not.'

'But you want to go to the museum by yourself?'

'No… I…' Mika retrieved the snatch of conversation from her memory. She'd been feeling out of sorts when she'd thrown that comment in. Aware that the next man in her life was not going to be Rafe… 'It's just that some people don't like museums, you know? I don't want to bore you.'

He was still holding her gaze.

'You would never bore me, Mika.'

Oh, help…that connection was still there, wasn't it?

And that look. She could fall into that, if she let herself.

Maybe she couldn't *help* herself falling…

'Same.' Mika felt her heart skip a beat. 'You're…good company, Rafe.' She had to break the eye contact because she felt suddenly, inexplicably, shy. She pulled her camera out of its case. 'It's…um…really nice to have a friend to do things like this with.'

'But you'd do it on your own if I wasn't here, wouldn't you?'

'I'd have to.' Mika focused on the terraced rows of lemon trees, the fruit glowing goldlike giant gems against the glossy, green foliage. 'But it's better when you have company. Makes it feel… I don't know…more real?'

'Mmm…' Rafe's nod was thoughtful. 'I get that. They say a problem shared is halved. Maybe a pleasure shared is doubled.'

She kept the camera in her hand as they carried on. There was so much pleasure to be found in this walk. They entered the valley into woodlands where the bird calls were the only sound to break the cool silence and the forest floor was a wash of pink from wild cyclamens. The ruins of the ancient paper mills were tall, mossy, concrete structures with haphazard holes where windows had once been, perched beside the river as it tumbled over huge boulders. The drama of one of the waterfalls they passed was enough to make them pause and sit beneath one of the massive old trees for a few minutes.

So much pleasure…and it was definitely doubled by having Rafe's company. More than doubled…

Mika could have simply sat here and soaked it in but she needed more than photographs to record the journey. She pulled her notebook from the pack Rafe had been carrying for her.

'What are you writing?'

'I'm adding to the research I did online. Putting the things I notice in as well. Like how gorgeous that carpet of flowers was under the trees. I won't have room to include every photo I take.'

'Include in what?'

'My article.'

'You're a *writer*? You never told me that.'

'That's because I'm not. Yet…' That very uncharacteristic shyness resurfaced. Mika didn't tell people her dreams. Was that because she didn't have anyone in her life that she wanted to share them with?

'I want to be a travel writer,' she said quietly. 'I'd like to earn my living by doing things like this all the time, instead of working in cafés.'

Rafe looked impressed. But then he frowned.

'You want to spend your whole life travelling? Never settling down anywhere?'

'Oh, I'll settle somewhere. I just don't know where yet. I know it will be near the sea because of my dolphin blood.' Mika smiled, hoping to make light of revealing something so personal. 'And I think it will be somewhere warm, because that way you can spend more time in the sea, but there's a lot of places in the world that fill those requirements—especially round here.' She closed her notebook and slipped it back into the pack. 'I'm killing two birds with one stone, here. When I find the place I want to be for ever, I think I'll know who I really am.'

Did everyone wonder who they really were at some point in their lives, or was this another extraordinary bond that Raoul had just found with Mika?

He wanted to tell her everything at that point. Who he was and why he was here. He could share his problems and maybe they would be halved.

Except they wouldn't be, would they? Okay, he could imagine that Mika would understand the need to reveal the strongest, most basic, layers of his personality so that he would know he had a foundation that would serve him well for the rest of his life—because wasn't she doing pretty much the same thing? She was searching for a layer he didn't need but one that was even more fundamental—a place where she felt she belonged.

But, if he did tell her the truth, she would realise he didn't belong here, in her world, like this. She might feel that the dream she had shared with him was insignificant in comparison to his future and she might show her prickles again—the way she had, inexplicably, in suggesting that she could go to the paper museum by herself.

And, if the prickles came out, the pleasure of this day would be dimmed and it was too good to spoil. The serenity of the dappled light in this forest had the echoes of a long and proud history in the ruins of the ancient mills but the bubbling river was timeless. A link to the future and a reminder that nothing stayed the same. Life moved on and changed...

He could accept that with a new sense of peacefulness in this moment and it felt really good.

Being with Mika felt really good, too. Maybe

it wasn't just their surroundings that made him feel so much closer to embracing his future. There was strength to be found simply in her company and in the way she faced life and made the most of every moment.

The sensation of feeling so close to another person's soul—as if his own could reach out and take the hand of hers—was a new thing for Raoul. As if he needed to see if it was real, he turned his head, to find Mika looking up at him. Her eyes were very serious but her mouth had the hint of a curve to it, as if she knew how deep his thoughts had been and that he was happy with where they'd taken him.

The need to connect on more than this weird, telepathic level was so strong Raoul could feel his head drifting. Tipping in slow motion until lowering it a little would be all that was needed to kiss Mika.

Did she know how overpowering the pull was? She didn't break the lock of his gaze and he could see a reflection of his own wonderment at how close it was possible to feel to someone else. And then her lips parted and he saw the very tip of her tongue touch her lower lip.

The shaft of desire was painful.

If ever there was a moment to test himself to see whether he could resist this overwhelming temptation, this was it.

Surely a kiss couldn't be such a big deal?

But it wouldn't stop there, would it?

If he wanted it *this* much, even a touch could be dangerous. What if it ignited something so powerful, he lost control of his best intentions? Exposed a weakness that could make him doubt himself even more?

He had to find out if he had the strength it would take to resist this. Closing his eyes helped because it was a shutter against how it made him feel to be holding Mika's gaze.

Forcing himself to move helped even more because he could get to his feet and walk away to put some distance between them. But the effort was draining and a good part of the peace he'd found ebbed as well. When they got home, he decided, he would have to find the concierge and ask about the availability of another room to rent. How could he sleep so close to her without having to fight that particular battle again and again? How many times could he fight it and not weaken to the point of giving in?

He knew Mika was following him but it was some time before he could break the silence.

'How many articles have you done already?'

'A few. I haven't tried to get any published yet, though. I need a really special one to send to the good magazines.'

'Maybe this will be the one?'

'Maybe…' Mika still had her camera out as they finally left the valley behind and came into the small village of Pontone. She stopped to take photographs of the wide, stone archway they walked through that had antique kitchen utensils and old woven baskets hanging from the walls. They found a picturesque café and sat, sheltered from the sun by big umbrellas, amidst barrels of bright flowers with tumblers of chilled home-made lemonade in front of them as they waited for the lunch they ordered.

'I love this,' Mika said, a while later.

'The salad? Me, too.' They had ordered *insalata caprese,* a salad of sliced mozzarella cheese layered with slices of the delicious bright red tomatoes grown locally, drizzled with olive oil and sprinkled with tiny basil leaves. It had come with crusty, just-baked bread and it had to be the most perfect lunch ever.

Mika laughed. 'It's my favourite lunch, but no, I mean all of this. This part of Italy. It's the closest I've come to feeling that it's my place.'

'Where else have you been?'

'I went to Scotland first, seeing as it's apparently where half my genetic history came from.'

'Ah, yes…you said your father was Scottish.'

'Mmm…'

There was a hint of something sad in her eyes. Something lost. Raoul couldn't remember his father very well, but he knew exactly who he was and what he looked like, and he could remember how important he'd been in his life. Knowing where your place was in the world was inextricably linked with family, wasn't it?

But Mika didn't have family. She was roaming the world in search of a link to something but, clearly, she hadn't found it in the birth place of the father she'd never known.

'You didn't like Scotland?'

Raoul loved the way her face scrunched up to reveal the impression she'd been left with.

'I loved the oldness. And the accent. I even loved the bagpipes but I didn't love the weather. It was too cold and the sea was so wild. I decided you'd have to be a bit mad to swim there so it wasn't ever going to be *my* place.'

'Maybe you need people to make it feel right. When you find your special person, you'll make a family and then the place will be yours. And theirs…for ever.'

Mika shook her head and her voice was quiet. Cold, almost. 'I'm never going to get married.'

'Why not?' The thought of Mika growing old alone was shocking.

But she simply shook her head again—a warning that the subject was off-limits. 'It's just not going to happen. I've learned that I'm better off on my own.'

How had that lesson been learned? Raoul wondered, in the slightly awkward silence that followed. He wished he hadn't said anything, now, because they'd lost that easy flow of conversation. Could he fix it?

'What about New Zealand?' he asked. 'Doesn't that feel like your place?'

'I love New Zealand, don't get me wrong, but…there's something about the oldness of Europe that calls me.' Mika seemed as relieved as he was to forget that forlorn blip in the conversation and start again. She grinned, as if embarrassed by being fanciful. 'Maybe I lived here in a previous life.'

Maybe she had. Maybe Raoul had, too, and that could explain why he felt like he'd known her for ever. Why they had this extraordinary connection.

'There's still so much of the coastlines to explore, too. It's exciting...' Mika's face lit up. 'I want to go to the south of France. And Spain. And the Greek islands. And Sardinia and Corsica and...' Her hands were tracing a map of the Mediterranean in the air.

'And...' Raoul only just stopped himself adding *Les Iles Dauphins* to her list.

Mika's eyes widened as she waited for him to finish what he'd been about to say.

'And...you will,' he managed. 'You could be anything at all you really wanted to be, Mika, and...and you're going to be the best travel writer. Your passion will make the pages glow and everyone who reads your articles will want to go to those places. To be where you've been.'

He would want that.

She was smiling at him. A soft smile that had nothing of the characteristic cheekiness he had come to expect. This was the smile of someone basking in unexpected encouragement. Of having their dreams become a little more real because someone else believed in them too.

He would want more than to read her articles, Raoul realised. He would want to go to those places *with* Mika, not after her. And he could make it happen, so easily. He could choose almost any place in the world and the means of getting there would be sorted instantly. A helicopter, a luxury yacht, a private jet... There would be comfortable accommodation waiting at the other end, too, and Mika could have all the time she wanted to do the thing she loved doing, without the prospect of having to get back to a mundane job.

But would she want that?

And wouldn't it change how she saw a new place? Earning a day off, as they'd had to, to make this trip possible, made it so much more valuable. Exploring somewhere by having to use public transport and eating at inexpensive restaurants made everything so different.

Maybe Raoul wouldn't want to go back to having the best of everything so easily available. If he had the choice, perhaps he would choose to go to those places with Mika in the same way they'd set off today. On foot, with no more than a bit of spare change to rely on.

This longing for more days like today had nothing to do with the desire to touch Mika physically, although he could still feel that simmering in the glow of her smile. This was about what it was like simply to be in her company. To contribute to Mika's strength to achieve any dream she held...and to feel like he had someone walking alongside him as he achieved his.

Was this what real friendship was about?

...Love?

Was he falling in *love* with Mika?

No. That couldn't be allowed to happen.

They could be friends. Very good friends. But that was all.

Some people were lucky enough to marry their best friends but he wasn't going to be one of them. His future was mapped out and he couldn't imagine Francesca being his best friend.

He barely knew her. Oh, they'd spent time together—usually at formal occasions—and he knew how beautiful she was, and that she was intelligent and easy to talk to. He could fancy her, even—in the way that any man could fancy a gorgeous woman—but would he ever feel like this about Francesca? That helping her get everything she wanted out of life could be as important as his own ambitions?

He had to hope so.

Maybe Mika had been sent into his life to

teach him about what was really important in relationships.

Raoul would never forget this moment.

Or that particular smile…

'What time does the paper museum close?'

Mika blinked as if she had to drag her thoughts away from something that had nothing to do with the article she was planning to write. 'I'm not sure… I imagine we've got plenty of time.'

'Shall we head off now? Just to be sure?'

'Okay…'

Mika hadn't moved a muscle but something in her tone told Raoul that she was much further away from him than she had been a moment ago, when she'd been smiling at him.

It was an odd thing, this connection he could feel between them. Like the sun emerging from the screen of thick clouds, there were moments when it scorched him; then it would vanish again and the whole world felt so much cooler.

What created the clouds? Was it because he was getting hot enough to feel uncomfortable, so that he pulled them in for protection, perhaps?

Or did Mika feel the heat, too; and was she using them to hide behind?

Whatever was causing those clouds, they were a good thing, because it made this friendship manageable and it needed to be manageable because Raoul was nowhere near ready to risk losing it.

He thoroughly enjoyed the time they spent in the *Museo della Carta* that was housed in a wonderful thirteenth-century mill. Raoul was no stranger to museums and was, in fact, the patron of the largest in his own country; he had toured it many times, usually in the company of a large group local dignitaries and important contributors. He had to look fascinated even if he wasn't and remember to turn a little whenever he shook someone's hand or stopped to admire a new exhibit, so that the best photographs could be taken.

This was a new experience because, for once, he was less important than the exhibits and he found that he was watching Mika as much as the treasures on display, and that made him see things differently and in far more detail. He stared up at the huge wooden mallets that were powered by a hydraulic wheel that could beat rags of cotton, linen and hemp into a pulp.

He stood beside the ancient vat with its murky water that housed the pulp and watched

Mika crouch to take a close-up shot of the majolica tiles that lined the vat. Pale blue tiles, with red flowers and delicate green swirls for leaves. Would he even have noticed them if he'd been here alone?

'I'm going to write this up tonight,' Mika announced, as they waited for the bus to take them back to Positano. 'And I'll finish the one about the Footpath of the Gods.'

'I'll get out of your way,' Raoul told her. 'I'm going to find the concierge and see if there's another room available. That way, you'll get plenty of time to write without interruptions.'

The bus was approaching the stop but Mika didn't seem to notice. Her gaze had caught his and those clouds had evaporated again as instantly and mysteriously as they had on every other occasion.

This time, the heat felt different. It wasn't the burn of desire. It felt more like the kind of heat that came with the prickle of shame.

Mika knew exactly why he was going to find the concierge. He wasn't finding his own place to sleep in order to give her more space, he was doing it because he needed to get away from her. And she felt…rejected?

The bus seemed to bring the cloud cover

back as it jerked to a halt beside them and Mika turned away to climb on board.

Maybe it would be the last time he got to experience the heat of that connection.

That would be a good thing, wouldn't it? It would make it so much easier to step back into his own world and his own life when the time came and that wouldn't be very far away. A whole week of his month of freedom had vanished already.

But, if it *was* a good thing, why did it feel as if he'd just broken something rather precious?

CHAPTER FIVE

IT HAD BEEN one of *those* days.

Right from that first customer who'd put his hand in the air and clicked his fingers loudly enough to make Mika freeze as she hurried back to the pass to collect more plates for the table.

'I ordered my eggs to be poached, not fried.' He didn't look at Mika as he spoke. 'Take them back.'

'I'm so sorry, sir.' Mika picked up the plate. 'There's been a mistake. I'll get you a fresh plate.'

'Make it snappy. And I'll have another coffee while I'm waiting. On the house—it's the least you can do for messing up my order.'

'Of course.' Mika looked over her shoulder, thinking that Alain had probably heard the loud voice. His subtle nod told her that he had and his smile offered sympathy at her dealing with a rude customer.

The customer wasn't the only person Mika had to deal with. She knew she hadn't written the order down incorrectly but the person who'd made the mistake wasn't likely to admit it. Not this morning, that was for sure, when they were being run off their feet.

Sure enough, Gianni was furious.

'How could you get something so basic wrong?' he shouted. 'You think I have time to be cooking another full English breakfast when I've got orders coming out of my ears?' His spatula splattered oil on the dockets lining the rail above the grill.

He'd picked the wrong morning to have a go at Mika. It had already started badly when she'd opened her eyes to remember that she was alone in her room. That Rafe had chosen to be a lot further away from her. Had that been her fault? Had she said or done something to put him off her? She hadn't been able to think of anything. Quite the opposite, really, when she'd gone over and over everything they'd said during yesterday's outing.

Okay, she'd upset him by being offhand about whether she wanted his company to visit the museum, but they'd got past that, hadn't they? More than past it. She could swear that he'd almost kissed her when they'd been sitting under that tree by the waterfall. And the way he'd looked at her when he'd told her that he was so sure she would succeed in her dream of becoming a travel writer. As if he believed in her completely.

As if it was important to *him* that she did achieve her dream.

But having him use that dream as an excuse to find somewhere else to sleep felt like she was being punished for something that she didn't feel was her fault, and now it was about to happen again so this pushed a button harder than it might have otherwise.

'Have a look at the docket,' she told Gianni. 'I didn't write the order down wrong. You *read* it wrong.'

'Don't tell me how to do my job!' Gianni yelled. 'You want to come in here and start cooking? *Do* you?' He'd stepped away from the grill and by the time he fired his last, aggressive question he was right in her face.

Mika stiffened. She knew that Gianni wouldn't hurt her but there were huge buttons being pushed now and it took everything she had to control her reaction. Behind her, she could sense that Rafe had stopped loading the dishwasher. He was staring, probably horrified, at the altercation. The second chef hadn't blinked and he was now busy trying to rescue the food that Gianni had left unattended on the grill. Margaret took plates off the pass and vanished swiftly. Gianni's temper tantrums were nothing new and it was best for everybody not directly involved to carry on with their own jobs. There was no point in escalating things further so Mika tried to push past Gianni's arm to put the offending plate back on the pass. Hopefully he would calm down and do what had to be done to satisfy the customer.

But standing up to him had been a mistake. Gianni grabbed the plate before it got to the bench. Maybe it slipped out of his hands, or maybe he threw it. It didn't matter because the effect was the same. The sound of smashing crockery caused a sudden silence in the busy café and, from the corner of her eye, Mika could see Marco glaring from his table on the footpath.

Rafe was right beside her now and she could feel him bristling. Was he ready to defend her? She shot a warning glance in his direction and followed it up with a firm shake of her head. It would only make things a lot worse if Rafe said or did anything. This was between herself and Gianni. The more people that got involved, the worse the whole day would become for everybody.

'What's your problem?' Gianni shouted at Rafe. 'Can't find the broom? Can't do *your* job, either?' He threw his hands in the air. 'Why do I have to work with such *stupid* people? Nobody can do the jobs they're being paid for.' He turned back to the grill in disgust, narrowly missing a collision with his junior chef who was putting new plates on the pass.

'Service,' he said. 'Table four.'

Mika's table. He'd managed to add a replacement plate with poached eggs to the remaining orders going to table four. Mika let out a breath she hadn't realised she'd been holding. If Alain had already delivered the free coffee as well, this small crisis might be over.

Even the mess. Rafe might have a face like thunder but he had a broom and pan in his hand and was sweeping up the broken crockery and food as she collected the plates, balancing one on her arm so that her hands were free to hold the other two.

In the end, it was no more than a commonplace disruption to smooth service but it had set the tone for the day. All of Mika's least favourite tasks had appeared, one after the other. Having to return an incorrect order was the biggest but others were equally irritating. Like the group of middle-aged women who treated her like their personal servant for the duration of their visit, requesting fussy changes to every dish they ordered, more ice for their water and replacement cutlery for all when one of them noticed a smudge on the handle of a knife.

Then there were the unsupervised toddlers who'd been allowed to smear smashed avocado all over the table, laminated menus and the wooden spokes of two chairs and up-end the sugar dispenser so that the crystals crunched underfoot. Mika knew that cleaning this particular table in time for the next group of customers was going to be a mission that would have her running behind for a considerable length of time.

And now, when the end of her shift was finally in sight, she had a table of young men who were getting progressively more obnoxious with every order of drinks she delivered to their table.

Their attempts to grab her legs was something she was adept at avoiding but the verbal innuendoes were harder to shake off.

'Whatcha doing after work, cutie? We could show you a good time.'

Her smile was tight. 'Are you ready to order?'

'I know what *I'd* like to order...' One of the men licked his lips suggestively as he leered at Mika, his gaze raking her body from head to toe.

She gritted her teeth, her smile long gone. 'I can come back in a minute, if you need more time to decide?'

'Just bring us pizza. And more beer.'

'Yeah...*lotsa* beer.'

The sooner this group left, the better. By then it would be time for Mika's shift to end and she could escape and go for a swim, and maybe she could wash away the unpleasantness of this entire day.

But would she be walking home alone? Back to the silent room she now had all to herself again? Would Rafe decide she might need the space to go swimming by herself, too?

The hollow feeling inside her chest was the worst thing about this bad day.

She was missing him.

If she was honest, she'd started missing him at the bus stop in Amalfi yesterday when he'd dropped that bombshell about finding the concierge and arranging a room for himself. She hadn't ended up doing any of the writing she'd planned to do. Instead, she'd relived every moment of their day together. Tried to second-guess every glance or remembered tone of voice. Tried—and failed—to understand how she could be so drawn to someone who didn't feel the same way.

It was Rafe who had needed the space—that much was clear.

She'd hardly seen him at work today, either, except for the incident of Gianni's outburst, when she'd made it clear she wouldn't welcome his involvement. Had that been why he'd seemed so preoccupied every time she'd been near the pass? Why he'd kept his back to her, intent on loading or unloading the dishwasher whenever she was depositing a pile of crockery? Why he'd been outside, in the alley for his break at a completely different time from her own? Had she offended him again, the way she had when she'd tried to push him away just a little bit by suggesting he didn't have to go to the museum with her?

When she thought about that, she realised it had been a forlorn effort to protect herself because she knew how much she was going to miss him when he disappeared from her life as suddenly as he'd entered it.

But all she'd achieved was to find herself missing him already, when he was still here. How stupid was that?

It had confirmed something, though. She needed to protect herself. If it felt this bad with him still here, how much worse was it going to be when he was gone for ever?

At least she hadn't fallen in love with him because Mika instinctively knew that that would make the missing unbearable. Not that she had any real evidence to base it on because she'd never been in love. Not the kind of love she'd seen other people experience, anyway. Mika was confident that that would never happen to her because life had taught her both to rely only on herself and to avoid anything that made her more vulnerable than she already was.

Falling in love with someone was to make yourself ultimately vulnerable, wasn't it?

She'd told Rafe that she would never marry and have a family of her own and she believed that. How could she chase a dream of something like that when she had no idea what shape it really was? She wasn't looking for her *person*. A home that she could call her own was the closest she was going to get to finding her place in the world.

This was a physical reawakening, that was all. An attraction that might have been enough to break down a very big barrier, if Rafe had been interested.

The messages she'd received on that score were mixed, to say the least, and Mika didn't like feeling confused.

Feeling rejected was even more of a downer.

She delivered pizzas to the table of young men and followed that up with another order of their drinks, avoiding their wandering hands and letting their crude comments become no more than the background buzz of a busy café. As soon as they'd gone, she could wipe down their table and she'd be finished for the day.

Would Rafe be due to finish then, too?

Maybe she should give him some more of that space and not even check to see if his shift was going to finish close enough to hers for it to be only friendly for one of them to wait so they could walk home together.

He knew she'd be going for the usual swim.

If he chose not to join her then at least she'd know for sure that whatever had been gathering between them was not going to go any further. She could start pulling herself together, then. She'd been fine before Rafe had come into her life. It was ridiculous to be afraid of how lonely she might be when he left.

The anger had been building all day.

How did someone like Gianni think he had the right to put people down like that? Mika wasn't stupid. Neither was Raoul, but the bad-tempered chef had left them both feeling at fault for a situation and its consequences that Raoul was quite sure had been the result of the chef's lack of attention to detail. Part of him had wanted to put everybody in their place. To reveal his identity and use the power he could summon with a click of his fingers that could potentially change the lives of these people. To get the chef fired. Provide Mika with enough money to let her achieve her dreams without having to put up with any of this kind of abuse.

And the way she'd put up with Gianni's tantrum hadn't been the only thing he'd noticed today.

She'd told him that you got to see the worst

of people in a job like this and she hadn't been wrong. Raoul could see out into the café when he collected pans from the chefs or replaced water carafes and glasses on their shelves. He'd seen people clicking their fingers to get Mika's attention. A group trying to sit down at a table she was trying to clean had glared at her as if it was her fault there was sugar or salt that had to be swept up before the table could be wiped clean. And he'd seen a low-life make a grab for her legs as she'd leaned over the table to deliver tall glasses of beer.

It wasn't right that someone like Mika had to put up with being treated like this because she needed a job to live and she just happened to be so far down the pecking order.

Because she was vulnerable.

He hadn't been allowed to stand up for her this morning as she'd faced Gianni's wrath and he'd thought he understood why, even if he didn't agree with it. Hospitality workers were easy to replace and Marco probably wouldn't have thought twice about firing them both if he'd faced the prospect of losing a good chef who'd be far harder to replace. He couldn't do anything about the way people treated her in the café, either, but it fed the anger. Maybe he was angry with himself, too, that he'd quashed the notion of revealing who he was because it would mean the end of this time of being so successfully incognito.

He'd seen that look in her eyes yesterday. That smile, when he'd offered her encouragement to believe in herself and her dreams. Had it been so special because it hadn't happened to her very often in her life? Was she more used to being treated as if she didn't matter? As if it was obvious she'd had to put up with whatever people felt like dishing out so many times in her life it didn't matter if they couldn't be bothered considering how she might feel?

She *did* matter, dammit. Raoul had wanted to help and her gestures had told him she didn't need his help. That she could look after herself, just the way she always had—except for that time when he'd first met her, when she'd been in the grip of something totally beyond her control.

She'd needed him then but he knew how hard it had been for her to accept his help.

To take his hand...

But this was her world and she knew what she was doing. Raoul had never been in a position of having to put up with being treated as being stupid or worthless. He didn't have to be in it now. He could walk out of here whenever he wanted to and step back into a life of privilege. A life where people looked up to him as being important even if he wasn't doing anything to earn that respect. It was the opposite end of the spectrum and it was an eye-opener, for sure.

Maybe he'd learned enough. He'd walked a few miles now, in the shoes of the invisible people, and it would change his perspective on many things. It would make him a better ruler. A better man. It wasn't that he hadn't always had a strong sense of what was right or wrong, but this experience of life as an ordinary person was sharpening his perception of the shades of grey within those boundaries.

It was wrong enough to anger him that Mika had to put up with people treating her so badly, even if she was tough enough to deal with it. When Raoul had caught a glimpse of the table of young idiots who were out to have a good time with whatever feminine company came within reach, it had been the last straw. He hadn't forgotten his impressions of Mika as a wild creature. Or the horrific thought that some man had hurt her in the past. She deserved protection even if she didn't think she needed it. She deserved to know that how she felt mattered.

That *she* mattered.

Raoul had had to fight the urge to march out of the kitchens and warn them to keep their hands and their crass comments to themselves. Or else...

Or else what?

Choosing to reveal his identity and throwing his power around would have been one thing. What if he got into a fight and maybe ended up getting arrested, being forced to admit who he was, and creating a scandal that would embarrass his entire nation? And what about his beloved grandparents? They'd sacrificed retirement to raise him and wait for him to be ready to take up his destiny and maybe doing that had contributed to his grandfather's failing health. How sad would it be to have the final days of their position as ruling monarchs marred by something so unfortunate?

He couldn't do that. Any more than he could act on the attraction towards Mika that was getting steadily more difficult to contain.

It would be easier to leave now.

Safer.

But would it also be cowardly? He'd already been tested in ways he had never imagined he'd be faced with in his quest to uncover his core strengths. If he left now, might he be running away from the opportunity to face an even more intense challenge?

Perhaps it was frustration more than anger that was making his gut churn today.

Frustration that his offer of help had been dismissed.

That he couldn't let Mika know how important she had become to him.

Most of all, that he wasn't being honest with her.

She'd revealed things to him that he knew she'd never told anybody else. Her search for a place where she felt she belonged—the idea that she would know who she was when she found a place to call home. Her dream of using her talents in photography and writing to make a new—better—life for herself.

But she knew nothing of him on such an intimate level.

What she thought she knew was no more than a pretence.

A lie…

He would tell her, Raoul decided as he finally hung up his apron for the day. He would tell her how he felt about her and why they could be no more than friends. He could offer her a new life, perhaps. Surely there would be a way to find her work within the vibrant tourism industry of his own country? Above all, he could thank her for giving him a perspective on life he would never forget, and they could talk about how best he could use his remaining time before he was due to report back and take up the reins of his future.

When was Mika due to finish her shift? The last glimpse into the café had shown her wiping down a very messy table after the rowdy group of young, male tourists had finally moved on.

But now Raoul couldn't see her anywhere. Margaret was looking after that section and Bianca had come in for the late shift.

'You looking for Mika?' Bianca handed an order form to Gianni. 'She just left a couple of minutes ago.'

Without him?

Raoul headed for the alley behind the café. The hope of having an honest conversation with Mika was fading rapidly but he'd created this new distance himself, hadn't he? He'd put up new barriers—literal barriers—in the form of the four walls of his new, private room in the boarding house.

Mika had felt rejected and she was running away. He couldn't blame her but, if he left things this way between them, it would haunt him for ever.

He needed to find her.

Had she taken the main street as her route home, detoured past the beach or marina to give herself a longer walk, or had she chosen the narrow back alleys that offered far more solitude?

The alleys, he decided. Because that would be the route he would take if he wanted a space away from other people after a bad day and knew it was the fastest route to get to the best part of the day—that swim...

He turned another corner, skirted a bank of rubbish containers and passed the open back door of a restaurant kitchen where he could hear a chef yelling at his kitchen crew. They were shouting back and the noise level should have been enough to cover up a much fainter cry but the sound caught something in Raoul's chest.

His heart...

He knew that sound even though it was so

muffled. He recognised that note of distress and it felt like a knife in his own chest.

The place it was coming from wasn't an alley, it was more like a hole in a wall—a bricked space that was a tiny courtyard with rear entrance doors to shops that were already closed and locked for the day.

And, right in the corner of the shaded space, was Mika.

Surrounded by the young men she'd been serving in the café. One of them was holding her from behind as she struggled, his hand over her mouth. Another was trying to put his hand up her skirt as she kicked out at him.

The impression of Mika's face was only in the periphery of Raoul's line of sight as he launched himself into the space but he didn't need a clear look to be painfully aware of what he would see.

He'd seen it before. The terror of a wild creature who had been trapped—unable to save herself from the dreadful situation she had found herself in through no fault of her own.

And this was worse than the vertigo that had left her stranded on a cliff side. This was un-thinkably horrific.

The frustration and anger that had been

building all day gave Raoul the strength to tackle four men without giving the odds a moment's thought. He had an advantage because they were so fixed on their evil intent that they hadn't seen him coming.

With a roar of pure rage that he didn't recognise as coming from his throat, Raoul grabbed the one who was lifting Mika's skirt by the scruff of his neck and hefted him into the air, before throwing him to one side. In almost the same motion, he swung his arm and let his fist connect to the jaw of one of the leering bystanders.

A blow to the side of his own head blurred his vision and seemed to intensify the sounds around him. The swearing of the thwarted attackers still on their feet and trying to defend themselves. Groaning from the one still on the ground where Raoul had thrown him. A scream from Mika as the man restraining her shoved her aside viciously. More raised voices as other people came running. From the corner of his eye, Raoul could see white aprons that suggested it was the staff from the nearby restaurant who had been alerted to the trouble and he caught the impression of them being pushed, and falling as the young men decided to make a run for it, but he didn't turn his head as he leapt forward with his arms outstretched to catch Mika before she fell and hit her head on the cobbled ground.

He had only held her hand before this moment and he remembered the trembling within the gentle circle of his fingers.

This time he was holding her entire body as tightly as he'd ever held anybody and he could feel the shuddering of someone who'd been pushed past the brink of fear.

Oh, God…had he been too late?

'Did they…? Are you…?' He couldn't bring himself to say the words, and Mika clearly couldn't say anything, but she knew what he was asking and she was shaking her head forcefully. Letting him know that he had been in time to stop the attack.

Just…

The restaurant staff were picking themselves up. More people were gathering in the narrow street. The chef was shouting for someone to call the police and a waitress stepped closer.

'Is she all right? Can I help?'

Mika was shaking her head again, curling closer within the fold of Raoul's arms. He heard her stuttered words and bent his head.

'Home...' she whispered. 'Please...take me home...'

She was so small, it took no effort to scoop her off her feet and into his arms. She wrapped her arms around his neck and clung like a child.

Raoul pushed politely through the worried onlookers.

'She's okay,' he told them. 'I'll look after her.'

'Who is she?' someone asked. 'The police will want to talk to her.'

'She's my friend,' Raoul told them. He straightened his back, instinctively calling on the kind of presence that he might have had if he'd been arriving at a royal function. He was in control and he expected it to be respected. 'She's safe.'

The crowd parted. In silence, they made space for him to carry Mika onto the open street and carry on up the hill.

He could have put her down then but he didn't want to.

This time, he wasn't going to let her go.

Even when he got to the boarding house and into her room he still didn't let her go. He sat down on the couch he'd slept on for those first nights and he cradled her in his arms and let her cry until the shuddering finally ebbed and he could feel her fear receding.

How ironic was it that Mika could feel so safe with a man's arms around her? When her worst nightmares of men touching her again had come so terrifyingly close actually to happening?

But this was Rafe.

And this felt like the safest place she had ever been in her entire life.

More than that.

Would she ever feel safe again if he wasn't in her life?

Missing him wasn't something that she could protect herself from and it wasn't something that was ever going to get easier. Given her lifestyle, it should be something she had become very used to, but when Rafe left it was going to feel like he was taking a big part of her with him.

Even if she hadn't fallen in love with him.

As calmness won over the shaking and she could breathe without triggering a sob, Mika felt something like a wry smile gathering strength somewhere deep inside.

Who was she kidding?

She might have been in denial about the process of falling but she already loved this man. That physical reawakening had come in the wake of finding someone who had touched her soul.

Someone she could trust.

Her breath came out in a sigh this time instead of a sob. She could find words finally.

'You did it again.'

His arms tightened around her. 'I wanted to kill them. Are you sure they didn't hurt you?'

Mika swallowed hard. 'They would have. If you hadn't found them.' She tilted her head. 'How did you find them? I knew as they dragged me in there that nobody would be able to see from the street.'

'I heard you. Just the faintest sound but I knew it was you. I think my heart heard you rather than my ears.'

Mika could feel tears prickle behind her eyes again but these were very different tears from those in the aftermath of fear.

She would remember those words for the rest of her life. They had to be the most romantic words she had ever heard.

Had Rafe just told her that *he* loved *her*?

It felt like he had.

One of those tears escaped and she could feel it rolling slowly down until it caught on the side of her nose. Rafe had seen it, too. He used the pad of his thumb to brush it away.

'It wasn't the first time something like this has happened to you, was it?'

Mika blinked, shocked. 'How did you know that?'

Silly question… Somewhere along the line, they'd had one of those lightning-fast, totally private conversations. Like the one where he'd asked if she would be okay sitting beside the view of that drop to the sea and had told her that he would change the arrangements if that would help.

He'd seen her fear even though she thought she'd kept it so well hidden. Had it been that moment she'd pulled away and headed for neutral ground after she'd seen the attraction in his eyes when they'd been sitting on the pontoon?

No. Maybe it had been there right from the start. When he'd touched her and she'd panicked and kicked his backpack over the side of the cliff.

It didn't matter. He knew. And, while it made her heart rate skip and speed up, it didn't make her feel any less safe that he knew.

'This was worse,' she whispered. 'There were more of them…and they were strangers.'

She felt the sudden increase in tension in Rafe's body.

'You *knew* him? Last time?'

Mika swallowed, closing her eyes against the shock she could see in his eyes. 'He was my boyfriend. But I didn't know how angry he could get. That he would think nothing of hurting me…that he would come after me when I tried to get away and force me to…to…'

Rafe's arms tightened around her and Mika could feel his cheek pressed to the top of her head. Then she felt his head turn and she could feel his lips on her hair. A slow, tender press that felt like a deliberate kiss of comfort.

For the longest time, they were silent. Mika knew she didn't have to go into the horrible details. That she didn't have to uncover those dreadful memories and make them fresh again.

It was Rafe who broke the silence.

'I think you're wrong,' he said softly. 'I think what happened to you before was worse than what happened today.'

Mika nodded slowly. 'Because you saved me…'

'No. Because you were betrayed by someone

you thought you could trust. Someone that was supposed to care about you and keep you safe.' His breath came out in a sigh. 'I'm so sorry that happened to you, Mika. I'm not surprised you don't trust men.'

Her eyes snapped open. It was important that she could see Rafe. That he could see her.

'I trust *you*,' she said quietly.

'I care about you,' Rafe said. 'You're safe.'

It seemed like the most natural thing in the world that he would kiss her again to seal the truth of those words. It was a gentle kiss but it stirred up everything that had been woken and waiting in Mika's body.

The fear and bad memories were becoming a distant memory. *This* was what mattered. This moment.

This man that she *could* trust.

Her heart was beating wildly as she shifted in his arms. There was one way, she realised, that she could put not only today's horror but the memories that had kept her trapped for so long behind her for ever.

One thing that could restore her faith that there were good men in the world and, amongst them, one that she could trust with not only her heart but her body. If she was brave enough…

'Rafe?'

The subtle quirk of those dark eyebrows was enough to tell her he wanted to hear her question.

'Would you do something for me? Please? Something that will really make me feel safe?'

His eyes darkened. 'Of course. What is it?'

Mika licked suddenly dry lips. The words were so hard to get out that they emerged in no more than the ghost of a whisper.

'Make love to me...'

CHAPTER SIX

FOUR TINY WORDS.

How could they be enough to make it feel as if the bottom of Raoul's world had simply vanished?

As if he was falling and there was nothing he could find to catch hold of and save himself.

He'd started slipping without even realising it was happening. Touching his lips to Mika's head. That gentle kiss on her lips. He'd stepped over a boundary and now he had the choice of which direction his next step was going to take him. He'd been right in thinking that kissing this woman was always going to be more than a small thing. That it would unleash a desire unlike any he'd ever experienced before. Physical control was still possible, of course. He wasn't an animal—like those brutes who'd captured

Mika this afternoon. He could stop, if that was the right choice.

This was it.

The challenge that was going to tell him who he really was. What his values really were and whether he was made of the right stuff to rule a country in the best interests of the many thousands of people who would be trusting him to do the right thing.

He'd convinced himself that resisting the attraction he felt towards Mika was that test so why, in this moment after those words had been uttered, and it felt like time was holding its breath, did it really so utterly *wrong*?

As if he didn't really have a choice at all?

Again, he was reminded of when she had taken his hand, up there on the top of that cliff. Of when her trembling had finally ceased and he'd known she was trusting him.

He'd felt taller, then. Powerful in a way that had nothing to do with him being a prince but everything to do with who he was as a man. Nothing would have persuaded him to break that trust.

And, right now, Mika was trusting him with so much more than her hand. She was asking him to take hold of her whole body and, by doing so, he would still be leading her to safety, wouldn't he?

To a place where she could believe it was safe to trust a man. To let him touch her.

Was it so far-fetched to imagine that she was trusting him with her entire future?

Raoul was aware of the part of his brain that was reminding him of the challenge he'd set himself—to put aside his own desires in order to do the right thing—but what *was* the right thing in this case?

It was astonishing how fast a brain could work. How thoughts could coalesce into a split second of time.

If he refused Mika's whispered plea, would she ever have the courage to ask again?

This moment had come in the wake of Mika being forced to face her worst nightmare and now being in a space where she felt safe. With someone she trusted as the closest friend she had available.

It was a no-brainer to hope that this particular combination of circumstances would never happen again. He would never want Mika to be attacked or even threatened ever again.

And if he was really honest with himself—and wasn't the point of this journey he was taking to be exactly that?—the thought of Mika being this close to any other man felt wrong and he knew there was a part of him that would always be envious of that man.

He could feel the whole shape of the small, lithe body he had cradled in his arms. He could still feel the incredible softness of her lips against his own. Mika had no idea how much she was asking of him but Raoul had a very good idea of how huge this gift he could give *her* was.

It was something that nobody else could ever give her, because this moment would never happen again, and she would remember it for the rest of her life. A life that might very well be happier because of this gift.

The choice had already been made, Raoul realised, as he slowly dipped his head to touch Mika's lips again with his own, knowing that this time it was going to be with passion, not an intention to comfort.

He'd been right in that there really wasn't a choice to be made at all. This had nothing to do with whether he was fighting or submitting to his own desires.

This was the right thing to do.

For Mika.

Because he loved her...

* * *

Nothing else existed the moment Rafe's lips touched hers and it was nothing like the gentle comfort of that first kiss.

Mika could fall into the overwhelming spiral of feelings that were so much more than a blinding physical need. This was an expression of love, and the combination of what both her body and her heart were experiencing was more than Mika could ever have believed was possible.

Rafe was so gentle with her that Mika knew he would stop in an instant if she gave any indication that she was afraid, or that she'd changed her mind, but neither of those things was going to happen.

She'd been waiting her whole life for this—she just hadn't known it was possible.

This was why people took the risk of being ultimately vulnerable, wasn't it? Because sex could never be like this if you weren't in love with your partner.

Surely nobody else had ever felt quite like this, though? She already had that weird kind of telepathic communication with Rafe that meant an entire conversation could happen in a glance. Maybe it was a natural extension of that connection that meant that every touch said so much as well.

Which was why she could feel his initial hesitation—the edge of gentleness that was still there enough to suggest Rafe needed reassurance as much as she did that this was a safe thing to be doing. It was Mika who slipped her hands under Rafe's tee shirt, to feel his skin beneath her hands and encourage him to take it off. She started to unbutton her own shirt but Rafe caught her hands, catching her gaze at the same moment.

And it was then that everything seemed to come together. The attraction that had been sizzling between them for so long, the desire unleashed by those first kisses and what was being said in that glance.

That this was about so much more than sex…

Mika was aware of the moment when everything else ceased to exist for Rafe, as it had done for her , and she tipped her head back with a sigh as she felt him take over the unbuttoning of her shirt and then the touch of his lips on the swell of her breast. They could both let go now and see just how close to paradise this was going to take them.

And surely it was as close as anybody could ever get in this life?

Mika had no idea when her tears had begun or when they had stopped; she could only feel them cooling her cheeks as they dried as she lay, still within the circle of Rafe's arms, waiting for the moment when she could catch her breath again enough to speak.

And, when she could, there was only one thing to say.

'Thank you,' she whispered.

'Oh…' Rafe still had his eyes closed, and the sound was no more than a soft groan, but Mika could see the way Rafe's lips were curling into a smile. And then he opened his eyes to look straight into hers. 'Believe me, it was my pleasure.'

The smile made everything perfect. It brought Rafe the friend back into the body of Rafe the amazing lover.

It made this real.

Mika hung onto his gaze. There were more words aching to escape. Words she had never said to anyone. Ever.

Oddly, they were harder to get out than the extraordinary request she'd made that had led to this.

But she couldn't *not* say them. Even though they made something else scarily real.

How vulnerable she had just become.

'I...' It was that smile that made this possible. The smile that seemed to underline the warmth and humour in those gorgeous, dark eyes. 'I love you, Rafe.'

Something she couldn't begin to define flared in his eyes but then the lids came down to shutter them and Rafe pulled her more closely against his body. For the longest moment, he simply held her, and Mika could feel the steady thump of his heart against her cheek.

The silence continued for so long that Mika forgot she was waiting for him to say anything. The rhythm of his heart and the warmth of his skin, in the blissful aftermath of their lovemaking, were lulling her towards what promised to be a deep and dreamless sleep.

Or maybe not dreamless.

When Mika woke, it was completely dark and Rafe was sound asleep in the narrow bed beside her, his arm still cradling her head against his chest.

She could hear the words. A low rumble that still seemed to reverberate in every cell of her body.

I love you, too...

Had she heard those words with her ears or her heart?

Maybe it didn't matter. Mika pressed her lips gently against the soft skin at the base of Rafe's neck and then, with a sigh, let herself slip back into sleep.

Life could change in the blink of an eye.

Or over the space of one night.

The world felt different when Raoul woke in the morning. All his senses seemed to be heightened. He could smell the coffee Mika was brewing, having boiled the electric kettle on the only power point her room provided, and he felt more awake long before he tasted it. He could hear the trickle of the water as she poured it into the coffee jug and the tiny sound—a faint hum of pleasure—that Mika made as she glanced up to see that he was awake and acknowledged his company with a smile.

It was the most beautiful smile he'd ever seen. Mika was beautiful. Her skin seemed to glow this morning and he could actually *feel* the touch of her glance against his own eyes. Through his whole body, in fact.

Was *this* how being in love made you feel?

He'd waited until he was sure Mika was asleep in his arms last night before he'd echoed the words she'd said to him.

I love you, too...

They were dangerous words to say aloud because they carried a promise that he knew he would not be able to keep.

Last night had been a gift for Mika.

It hadn't occurred to him how much of a gift he was also receiving but, there it was, sitting inside his chest. Something huge, warm and comforting.

He knew exactly who he was.

A man who could feel this kind of love. Who could protect and nurture. Who could follow his instincts about whether something was the right thing to do, even though there were loud arguments against it, and trust those same instincts that were telling him it would be worth it, despite any inevitable consequences.

He was a man he could be proud of being.

And there was something even bigger that had brought him to this space.

Mika loved him.

She had no idea who he was or where he came from. She barely knew anything about him, but she loved what he was in this moment of time, and that had nothing to do with his elite position in life or his wealth. It was based entirely on who he was as a man.

A man worthy of being loved.

Would she still feel the same way when she found out the truth?

She had to know the truth. Was he really a man worthy of being loved if he was being dishonest?

On the other hand, wasn't he being more honest than he'd ever been in his life before? He had nothing to hide behind. Mika was seeing him as simply the person he was inside, without any of the trappings that were inescapable if you were a member of a royal family.

By a quirk of fate, he had escaped them completely, albeit temporarily.

With a huge effort, Raoul slammed a mental lid on that can of worms. He knew it was wrong—just as much as he'd known that giving Mika the gift of feeling safe to be touched had been right—and he was not impressed with himself for doing it, but he couldn't go down that track just yet.

He would break Mika's trust if he did and that would erase any of the magic that had happened last night.

It would be easy to persuade himself that this continued deception was to protect Mika but he knew he needed it for himself as well. This discovery was too important. This was what he'd set out on this journey to discover—who he was at the very core of his being—and he'd only just found it, this very instant.

He needed time. To hold this precious gift up to the light and look at it from every angle he could find. To revel in the beauty of its simplicity and its strength.

To make sure it was real…

'Hey, sleepyhead…' Mika's voice was a smile in itself. 'You'll need to hurry up if you want to have coffee and a shower before we go to work.'

Work.

Washing dishes. The most mundane of employment but even this felt completely different today.

Knowing that, at any moment, he might catch a glimpse of Mika coming to the pass to collect plates, or that she could arrive beside his sink to deposit dirty dishes and share a glance and a smile, made even the worst jobs of the day worthwhile. With his senses so heightened, he could actually hear her voice at times amongst the cacophony of customers chatting, dishes clattering and even the chefs arguing. And whenever they were close enough for their gazes to meet, and one of those silent, light-ning fast conversations to happen, he could feel a swell of what he could only identify as joy.

This was…happiness, that's what it was.

And, okay, it couldn't last—not in this form, anyway—but Raoul needed to hang onto every moment of it that he could because…

Because it felt perfect.

As though nothing else at all mattered.

Nothing else mattered.

There was nothing that could happen that day that could dent the astonishing joy that en-cased Mika like a private force field. Rude cus-tomers and crying babies, even the small dog that bared its teeth and snarled whenever she approached that table, did nothing to spoil her day. It made no difference that there were only snatched moments here and there when she ac-tually saw Rafe or could share a glance or a smile. He could have been a thousand miles away and it would have still felt as if he was right by her side.

It was just as well she was so good at her job because every task was being accomplished on an automatic level. Most of her head was filled with thoughts of Rafe. Thoughts that were more like sensations, really, that she could feel right down to the tips of her toes. A memory of his smile. The sound of his voice. The touch of his fingers or lips on her skin…

So this was what it was like to be in love.

It was extraordinary.

Crazy.

She barely knew him but that didn't seem to matter. In a way, it was exciting, because there was so much still to find out. She had taken the first steps on a journey she had never expected to take, but the unknown wasn't daunting, because she wasn't on this journey alone.

Okay…maybe it *was* daunting. There was a rollercoaster of emotions that came with such heightened awareness and, as the day wore on, the dips caught Mika when she was least expecting them. There were aspects of this that were quite possibly terrifying.

What if this wasn't real?

What if Rafe didn't feel the same way?

What if his holiday came to an end and he simply said goodbye and she never saw him again?

An answer to the disturbing whispers came

as their shifts ended and Mika found Rafe waiting for her outside the back door of the café.

'Time for a swim?'

'Oh…yes. I can't wait.'

'Neither can I.' Rafe held out his hand. 'Let's go.'

Maybe it was the way he took her hand, as if it was the most natural thing in the world to do. Or maybe it was his smile or the expression in his eyes. Whatever it was, it made Mika's fear evaporate.

If Rafe vanished from her life without a backward glance, she would have *this* for ever.

The knowledge that it was possible to feel like this.

As if life was perfect and only this moment mattered. That was what she needed to hold onto. This moment.

The future would happen, and it wasn't something she could control in the same way she had been controlling her life, because she had, for the first time in so long, chosen to open herself to being vulnerable. To allow someone else to hold the gift of her heart and her happiness.

CHAPTER SEVEN

THERE WAS NO race out to the pontoon today.

It was tempting to stay close to the rock wall, in fact, with the music from the bar right above them—to simply float in the deliciously cool water and play like other young couples always did here—but it felt too public. As if what they had discovered with each other was too new and special to be on display just yet. It only took a shared glance for that suggestion and agreement to be made and Mika had no idea whether it had been her idea or Rafe's. Not that it mattered.

They swam side by side this time, and their hands touched the side of the pontoon at the same moment. Their bodies bumped together as they sank into being upright, and Mika let go of the pontoon to wrap her arms around Rafe's neck and her legs around his waist as she lifted her face for the first kiss since last night.

For an instant, she was aware of a tiny hesitation on Rafe's part and the dip in that emotional rollercoaster was so fierce it felt like she was leaving her stomach behind as she fell. But then his lips softened on hers and she felt his legs move to keep them both afloat as he let go of the pontoon to wrap his arms around her. It was only a matter of time before the water washed over the top of their heads and they had to surface to breathe, but who knew that kissing under water could be so amazing?

The sea was Mika's ultimate comfort zone. To be in that space, with the added magic that being in love seemed to bestow on everything, made that fraction of time something that she knew she would remember for ever. This would be the moment that she could return to if she ever lost sight of how perfect life could be. This total embrace of the cool water that made the heat of Rafe's skin against hers so intense. How safe it made her feel to be within the circle of his arms. The blinding heat of passion that licked her whole body from just the touch of his lips and tongue.

It lasted for ever, but it was over in a moment, and ended with a tangle of limbs, some frantic kicking to get back to the surface and a lot of laughter as they both hauled themselves up to sit on the solid planks of the pontoon. Again, by tacit consent, they sat quietly to watch the sunset with Mika's head against Rafe's shoulder and his arm draped loosely over hers, his fingers covering her tattoo.

The sunset was as gorgeous as ever but Mika closed her eyes after a minute or two because she wanted to bask in this feeling of such astonishing closeness. It was hard to pinpoint where her body ended and Rafe's started—as if they were two parts of one being. How had she not known that she had been missing another part of herself? That she had never felt complete?

It was the movement of Rafe's fingers on her arm that finally distracted her. Purposeful movement of just a single finger that was tracing the peaks and troughs of the inked design.

'It's the sea, isn't it?'

'Yes. It's a Maori design. The sea—and the land—have a huge spiritual significance in Maori culture.'

'I get that. I come from a country of islands, too. The sea is everything.'

Mika's breath caught. Rafe never talked about where he came from. Or anything else about his past. The only thing she really knew was that he'd been left without parents early in his life—as she had. This was the start, then, of finding out about this man she had fallen in love with.

'What islands? Where are they?'

'Out there...' Rafe tilted his chin towards the expanse of the Mediterranean, now gilded rose-pink by the rays of the sun. He was silent for a long moment and then his words were so quiet Mika barely heard them. 'They're named after the creatures they're famous for. *Les Iles Dauphins.*'

'No *way*...' Mika sat up straight so that she could turn her head to stare at Rafe. His arm fell away from her shoulder and the connection between their bodies was broken.

He stared back at her, an oddly wary expression in his eyes, and weirdly Mika felt a chill run down her spine. She swallowed hard.

'How did I not know that a place like that existed?' Her fingers had gone to the charm around her neck. 'Why didn't you tell me before?'

That wariness was still there but it was softened as Rafe offered an apologetic smile. 'I guess it didn't seem important. I'm here. And you're here. Maybe I'm just living in the moment.'

Which was exactly what Mika had decided she needed to do. But questions were bubbling to the surface now and she couldn't hold them back.

'How far away are your islands? Do you live there now? How many dolphins are there?'

The curiosity in Mika's eyes was enchanting as her questions tumbled out like those of an excited child.

The moment of dread, when he had been sure she knew about his homeland and had suddenly made the connection and knew who he was, was evaporating.

He had taken the first step towards being really honest with her and it felt good. If he was gentle in the way he carried on, perhaps they could get to a place that would make their inevitable parting less painful.

He took a deep breath as he smiled back at her. 'They're not so far away but they're isolated enough to stay under the radar of the more usual tourist haunts. They're known as a tax haven. There's a thriving industry building luxury yachts. And the waters are a dolphin sanctuary. And, yes, I do live there now but I was away for quite a long time to go to school and university.'

'What did you study at university?'

'Oh…history. Politics. Environmental things…'

Mika's breath came out in a huff. 'Good grief…are you going to be a politician when you grow up?' She shook her head. 'I don't even know how *old* you are, Rafe.'

'I'm thirty-two.'

'Do you have a job?'

It was time to back off. 'I'm kind of between jobs right now. I wanted to try something different.' He'd had no idea, had he, of just how different that something was going to turn out to be?

Mika was grinning now. 'How's that working out for you, then?'

'I'm loving it.'

'But you're not going to be washing dishes when you go home, are you?'

'No.'

'What will you be doing?'

'Too many things, I expect.' He could feel the weight of those duties pressing in on him. The politics. The pomp and ceremony. The lack of personal space and choices. The sense of duty that would be ever-present…

The clock was ticking loudly now. This time was precious. He would never have anything like it, ever again.

Mika frowned. 'Are you a politician already?'

Raoul laughed. 'No…why?'

'Because you're so good at not giving a straight answer to a question.'

It really was time to distract Mika and there was a sure-fire way to do exactly that. By kissing her.

Or maybe he had wanted to distract himself. To remind himself of this extraordinary connection to another person that he had discovered and what it was teaching him about himself. That he wanted to buy a little more time simply to experience this.

Lost in the sheer pleasure of Mika's response, it was a surprise to find how brightly the lights of the bar on shore were shining. It told them how late it was getting but Raoul stole one more kiss. And then he held Mika's face between his hands.

'I don't want to think about my next job right

now,' he said softly. 'Can't we just have this time? Just for us?'

Despite the fading light, he saw the shadow that clouded Mika's eyes. But he also saw determination and a smile that made light of any misgivings she might have.

'Okay. But will you answer one more question? Honestly?'

Raoul's heart skipped a beat. 'I would never lie to you, Mika.'

But he had already, hadn't he?

No. He just hadn't told her everything. But what if her next question was the one that ruined this moment? He wasn't ready for that. Not yet.

These memories would have to last him for ever. Surely one more night with Mika wasn't too much to ask for?

That curiosity was still lighting up her face and it was encased in a warmth that made him feel like he could tell her anything and she would accept it. Would forgive him, even. It was a risk but, in that moment, he felt safe enough to take it.

'One question,' he managed. 'Go for it.'

But Mika's face scrunched into thoughtful lines. 'Can I have one question tomorrow, too?'

He had to laugh. 'That's your question?'

'Oh, no...' Mika was laughing too. 'That's not fair. It's not a real question.'

'Why not?'

'Because it's not about *you*...'

There was something shy in her eyes. She was asking to be allowed closer but not quite sure if that was something he wanted. Raoul felt a tiny pang, as if a hairline crack had just appeared in his heart.

'Okay. We won't count that question. And, yes, you can have another one tomorrow.'

'And one the day after that?'

Oh...how tempting was that? The idea of more days. And nights. Of more hours than he could count just to be with her like this...

Mika was nodding as though he'd already agreed to the plan. And she was smiling.

'In that case, I have my last question for today.'

'What is it?'

'Whose turn is it to buy dinner?'

The trouble with questions was that one was never enough.

One question could open a door but then you stepped through it and it seemed like you were in a corridor with more and more doors stretching ahead of you.

Even deciding on that one question was tricky. One minute Mika would know for sure what she was going to ask next, but then she would come up with the potential answer she might get and she would see all those new doors. And she wasn't at all sure she wanted to open them.

Like, if she asked whether he would be going home to his magical-sounding islands as soon as his holiday ended.

It didn't make any difference whether his answer would be positive or negative because there were other doors that might change her life completely if she walked through them.

Like the one that might open if she asked if he wanted her to go with him…

It was too soon to open a door like that. What if the answer was no? That would break the bubble they had found themselves in now and Mika couldn't bear to do that. She had never been this happy.

Rafe hadn't moved back to his own room. Last night, when they'd caught the bus back to Positano after the swim she would always remember for that underwater kiss, he'd stopped when they'd found a pharmacy that was still open. They'd both been a little embarrassed by the purchase of condoms but Mika had been secretly thrilled. The love-making wasn't about to stop.

The fact that she was so happy about that was unbelievable. Was it only a couple of weeks ago that she had been so sure she would never let another man that close to her again? Her life had changed and her future was looking completely different.

Better.

Okay, they'd taken a stupid risk last night, but the moment had been too intense to think about something as premeditated as contraception and the odds were fortunately low enough for both of them to ignore, apparently. Well, not entirely ignore, because they'd had one of those silent conversations that had taken all of a heartbeat the moment that Rafe had picked up the box in the pharmacy and his gaze had met hers.

Is it too late?

It was a safe time, I'm sure of it.

Are you sure? You'd tell me, wouldn't you? If...

Yes, of course I'd tell you. Stop worrying... I'm sure...

She *was* sure but continuing that risk was definitely unacceptable. Mika hadn't yet found the place she would be content to call home. Getting pregnant would bring her journey to a grinding halt. Worse than that, it might scare Rafe so much that he would vanish from her life—the way her own father had. She would probably have to retreat to a place where life was familiar enough not to present extra challenges and that place was half a world away from where she was now.

With Rafe.

She watched as he paid for his purchase. Seeing his profile reminded her of that photo she'd taken the first evening they'd gone swimming together. Shifting her gaze, she took note of the printing machine in the corner of the pharmacy. She could pop in here with her camera card on a break from work and nobody would notice. How good would it be to have a copy of that photo that she could hold in her hand? A small, private thing to treasure.

One day, she would confess and check that he didn't mind, but that was an insignificant question compared to so many others.

So many questions that piled up in a corner because it was too hard to put them in an order of priority and appropriate times to ask were few and far between. There was never a chance to ask a meaningful question while they were at work together and, lying in his arms at night, random conversation was the last thing that came to mind.

This place—in this particular part of the world, with Rafe—was too good for Mika to want to risk changing a thing. In the end, she actually forgot to ask a personal question that day in the precious time between work and bed.

And she decided not to the day after that. Rafe seemed happy to be taking a day at a time—just for them—so maybe she needed to do that, too.

And it was enough for a few days. More than enough. This was a healing time for Mika and every day she felt safer as a little bit more of her protective shell crumbled and fell away. There were no tears in the wake of love-making now. She was becoming more playful and often there was teasing and laughter that added something completely new. Rafe was not only the most amazing lover she had ever found but he was her best friend as well.

The sense of something so solid between them made those doors far less daunting. So much so that there came a point, when a personal question came out so casually, it felt as natural as taking hold of Rafe's hand whenever they walked somewhere, like to the beach or home from work.

'What did you do?' she asked. 'In your last job?'

'I was a helicopter pilot.'

Mika's jaw dropped. His answer had come so automatically she knew he wasn't kidding but it was the last thing she had expected him to say. As far-fetched as him being an astronaut, perhaps. Or a brain surgeon.

'A commercial pilot?'

'No. I was with the military. We ran a rescue service as well.'

'Did you save people?' Mika smiled as she shook her head. 'Silly question. Of course you did. You've saved me twice already—it's second nature for you, isn't it?'

'I wouldn't say that.'

'Will you go back to a job like that?'

'No.'

'Why not?'

'I have another job waiting for me. That's why I needed a break. I wasn't sure how ready for it I am.' He squeezed Mika's hand. 'Are we going for a swim today?'

'Are you trying to change the subject?'

The discomfort in his glance confirmed her suspicion and Mika felt a chill run down her spine. What was he hiding? She hated the sudden tension that seemed to increase the heat of the late-afternoon sun enveloping them.

Her mouth simply ran away with her next question.

'You're not *married*, are you?'

'No.' Her hand was jerked as Rafe stopped in his tracks.

'Have you been in jail recently?'

His breath came out in an incredulous huff. '*No.*' But he was smiling as he tugged her into his arms and silenced her with a kiss. 'Enough questions, already...'

Mika could feel both the need to ask anything and that odd chill of premonition evaporating in the wake of his kiss.

'Okay...but I get to ask another question tomorrow.'

'Maybe.'

'You can't say that. You agreed.'

'Not exactly. And, even if I did, there's a problem with that arrangement.'

'Which is?'

Rafe's smile widened into a grin. 'You can't count.'

They started walking again and a welcome puff of a sea breeze lessened the heat around them. Or maybe it was that the tension had been blown away.

Mika's lips quirked. 'How many times will you make love to me tonight, Rafe?'

'One.'

She glanced up to catch his gaze and they both laughed.

'So I'm not the only one who can't count, then...'

CHAPTER EIGHT

IT WAS RAFE'S idea to do something special on their next day off.

The day was still early and deliciously cool but the clear sky suggested that being close to the sea would be the best way to enjoy the rest of it. Waiting for a beachside café to open for breakfast, they wandered past the main beach in Positano where the deck chairs for hire were already being set up in orderly rows, colour-coded for the businesses that owned them, and they began to explore the marinas where boats of all sizes and shapes bobbed gently on their moorings.

It was Rafe who spotted the sign advertising a day trip out to the island of Capri. The cost was an extravagance in Mika's opinion but Rafe persisted as they retraced their steps to find coffee.

'You want to see it, don't you? It would make a great subject for one of your articles.'

'I would love to see it. I've been intrigued ever since I saw the outline of those rocks in the distance.'

'The *Faraglioni*? The Three Spurs? They're very distinctive. Did you know you can go right though the gap in one of them?'

'No…really?'

'If we find the right boat, it'll be part of the trip.'

'It's too expensive.'

'It would be my treat. And you need a new subject. You've finished your articles on the Footpath of the Gods and the Valley of the Ancient Mills now, haven't you?'

Mika caught her bottom lip between her teeth. 'I emailed them last night.' She scrunched her nose. 'I can't believe I took your advice and sent them to *National Geographic* and *Lonely Planet*. They only take the best.'

'It's a good thing.' Rafe squeezed her hand to make her pause and then dipped his head to kiss her. 'Always start at the top. Why settle for less if you don't have to?'

'Mmm…' The sound was a sigh of happiness in the wake of that kiss. 'Okay…if you're sure. But you could buy a lot of new clothes with that kind of money. I'll bet you haven't replaced half of what you lost when I kicked your backpack over that cliff.'

'Ah, but I've learned how little you actually need to survive,' Rafe said quietly. 'And, more than that, how good life can be when you keep things simple.'

The look in his eyes told Mika that *she* was the reason life was so good for him right now and the bubble of joy that caught in her throat exploded to send ripples of pleasure right through her body.

'I'll have to go home to get my camera. And my notebook.'

'We've got an hour or so before the boat leaves. I'll go back and make sure we can get tickets while you fetch your camera. We'll still have time for a quick breakfast. Let's meet at the café beside the bus stop.'

Excitement was chasing joy now. 'Race you, then.' Mika stood on tiptoes to press another kiss to Rafe's lips. 'I'll be back here first.'

She wasn't, because she took a little extra time to throw their sunhats and some sunscreen into her small backpack, but it didn't matter, because Rafe had ordered coffee and croissants and had the tickets in his hand that were a passport to a new adventure. Mika couldn't wait. She was first on the boat to ensure the best position to take photographs and already had her camera in her hands as more and more people climbed aboard. The powerful launch took them swiftly up the coast and Mika started taking a series of shots as the massive spurs of rock the island was so famous for came closer and closer.

The side of the boat was not going to be the best place to record the experience of going through the gap of the middle spur, so Mika edged her way through the group to get to the back. A young man, holding a remarkably similar camera to her own, made space for her beside the rail.

'Nice…' He tilted his head as he looked at her camera. 'It's a D4, isn't it?'

'Yes. What's yours?'

'A D5. It's the latest.' He sounded English. And very confident. 'The best.'

'Wow…'

'I need it for my job. I'm a pro.' He grinned at Mika. 'I'm James.'

'Nice to meet you. I'm Mika.'

The boat was slowing, coming closer to the

arched hole. Mika readied her camera but took a sideways glance at her new companion. He was going to get very hot today in those tight, black jeans and tee shirt but he certainly looked professional. The huge lens he had on his camera at the moment made her think of paparazzi.

The passage through the gap was exciting, with the roll of the sea and the height of the ceiling of rock overhead making the walls feel closer than they probably were. Mika tilted her camera, trying to capture it all.

'You need a wide-angle lens.'

'It's on my list. I'm saving up.'

Mika lowered her camera as the boat picked up speed, turning her head to see where Rafe was in the crowded boat.

'Hang out with me for the day and you might earn enough for any lens your heart desires.'

'What?' She turned back swiftly. 'How?'

'There's a rumour that there are some big names coming to the island today for a spot of shopping.' He tapped the side of his nose. 'Can't say who, but they're the hottest ticket there is right now. Get a good shot, and you could sell it for serious cash.'

So he *was* paparazzi. Mika took a step back, shaking her head. 'Thanks for the offer, but

I'm spending the day with my boyfriend.' Another glance showed her that Rafe was still in the spot she'd left to come to the back of the boat. And he was watching her. Or, rather, he was staring at James.

James was staring back. 'Lucky guy,' he said. 'My loss.'

'Who was that?' Rafe asked when Mika got back to his side.

She shrugged. 'He said his name was James and he's a professional photographer. Apparently there's a movie star or someone going to Capri today and he wants to get a shot he can sell.' She made a face to express her distaste. 'He said I could make big money if I hung out with him for the day.'

A glance over her shoulder revealed that she was still an object of interest for James. Or was it Rafe he was staring at? Impossible to tell now that he had sunglasses on, and he turned away as soon as Mika spotted him. Or, rather, he waited a heartbeat before he turned away. And he was smiling. Did he want her to know that he was still watching? That he was enjoying whatever game he thought he was playing?

'We picked the wrong day for this, I think.'

There was a note in Rafe's voice that Mika

had never heard before. He sounded angry. Disgusted, even.

'Why?' Anxiety formed an unpleasant knot in her stomach. She didn't want this to be a 'wrong' day. She wanted a day like their walk through the valley of the ancient mills when that feeling of being connected to Rafe had become so incredibly strong. He'd fought the attraction, though, hadn't he? He had come so close to kissing her but had pulled away—so much so that he'd moved out of her room.

But now…everything had changed. If they were totally alone in a beautiful place, and returned to that kind of space where there was nothing else but that connection, would it grow even more? And, if it did, where would it take them? Could she ask the questions that would open the scariest doors of all?

Maybe she wouldn't need to ask them. Maybe he would tell her that he didn't want to stop sharing his life with her. Ever…

But, right now, he was scowling.

'Paparazzi are like wasps. When one gets attracted, you know there'll be dozens more. I hate them.'

Mika blinked. 'Hate' was such a strong word—as if he had personal experience of something extremely unpleasant. Or did he hate the principle of privacy being violated? That was more likely. Despite how little she still knew about him, Rafe was clearly a very private person.

And that was fine. Privacy was exactly what she was hoping they could find today.

'We won't hang around the shops,' she said. 'Look, I've got a brochure. There's a map. We could go walking and see something historic. Like this—the *Villa san Michele*. That looks amazing.'

Their boat wasn't the only one docking at Capri and the streets were already crowded. When they made their way to the funicular train to ride up the side of the cliff to the *piazetta*, they were urged on to squeeze in with dozens of other tourists.

Maybe Rafe was right, Mika thought, as she was jostled hard enough to cause momentary alarm. They *had* picked the wrong day for this. But then his arm went around her shoulders and his was the only body she was pressed against, and she felt safe again. They emerged into the square and the crowd thinned as they dispersed towards the cafés and shops. Mika breathed a sigh of relief and unfolded the brochure she was still holding in her hand.

'Let's find the road we need. Looks like the *Via Acquaviva* to start with and then the *Via Marina Grande.*'

'How long will it take to get to the villa?'

'It says about forty-five minutes.'

'It might be a good idea to buy some water and something to eat.' Rafe still sounded out of sorts, and he wasn't looking at Mika. He seemed to be scanning the crowds around them and wasn't happy with what he could see.

'Okay. My turn to pay this time.' Mika touched her shoulder to slip off the strap of her camera case and retrieve the euros she had tucked into a side pocket for easy access. 'Oh, my God…'

'What is it?' Rafe was looking at her now, his brow furrowed with concern. 'What's wrong?'

'My camera… It's *gone…*'

'You didn't put it in your backpack?'

'No. It was over my shoulder. I had it when I got on the train.'

When she'd been jostled hard enough almost to fall.

'You must have dropped it. We'll go back to the station and see if someone's handed it in.'

Mika's sinking heart told her that this was probably too much to hope for. The head shaking of the train officials was bad enough. Being given a lecture about being wary of pickpockets in tourist destinations was worse. She left her details with the officials and a woman assured her that she would pass the information to the police in case the camera turned up elsewhere.

The shine had been taken off the day and it seemed like they were both out of sorts now.

'I'm sorry,' Rafe said. 'Your camera can be replaced but you won't get photos today. You've saved your earlier pictures, haven't you?'

Mika nodded. They were all safely on her laptop. The most precious one of all—that she'd printed into a passport size the other day at the pharmacy—was tucked into the wallet she'd left at home for safekeeping.

And, yes, the camera could be replaced but how long would it take her to save up that kind of money again?

It was a setback, one that could very well ruin this day, but Mika couldn't afford to let that happen—not when she didn't know how many more days like this she would have with Rafe. Where they could find the right time and place that would make it natural to talk about what the future might hold…

With a huge effort she pushed the negative effects of her loss to one side.

'You know what?'

'What?'

'I've still got my notebook. I can come back and get photos another time. Maybe one of my articles will sell and that'll be enough to buy a new camera.'

Raoul could see the effort Mika was making. He knew how hard it was for her and he loved her for that courage and determination in the face of adversity.

That camera was precious. She had worked so hard for it and it represented her dream of a better future.

He would replace it for her. Not only the camera, but he would get every type of lens available as accessories—a tripod too, perhaps, and a beautiful case to carry everything in. He could have it gift-wrapped and delivered as soon as he got home.

When he'd left Mika behind…?

He didn't want to think about that. Not today, when it might be the last day they got to spend together like this. While they were both still invisible as far as his real world was concerned.

In the meantime, he needed to encourage her. To make them both feel better. His own mood still left a lot to be desired. The day had soured for him when he'd seen the way that photographer had tried to hit on Mika. It hadn't been as simple as jealousy, though, had it? His instincts had been validated by knowing that James was a paparazzo. One of the army of watchers that had never been far away for his whole life—a symbol of why he'd never really known what he'd needed to know about himself because he'd always had to be what others expected him to be.

He could be who he really was today, though. Not being able to protect Mika from that theft rankled but he could fix that, in time. For now, perhaps all he could do was offer comfort.

'Someone might still hand it in. We could check in at the police station on our way back.'

A police station was the last place Raoul wanted to go, though. What if they wanted his ID and awkward questions led to him having to confess the truth?

Mika's gaze was steady. Given the way they could communicate, it was more than likely that she could sense his reluctance. Was that why she was shaking her head?

'They've got my details. It's pretty obvious the theft was deliberate so I doubt it'll be handed in anywhere.' She shrugged. 'It's rotten but I don't want it to spoil our day. Let's try and forget about it.'

Her smile was pure Mika, with that edge of feisty cheekiness, but there was a hint of apology in her eyes.

'Have you got enough money for some water and a sandwich or two? Mine was in the camera case.'

Raoul could only nod because he didn't trust himself to speak for a moment. It summed up so much, didn't it? How much he loved her zest for life and the courage she displayed in living it. How little she knew about him to think that paying for a simple meal might be stretching his resources. How much she loved him, that she didn't want their day to be spoiled.

Escaping the crowds of the *piazzetta* and the streets of boutique shops that were luxurious enough to attract the kind of customers that the paparazzi loved to follow was a huge relief but, for a long time, their walk was silent and a little sombre.

Maybe it was the magic of the quiet, residential streets with their pretty gardens and wafting scents of lemon trees and lavender. Or maybe the increasing peacefulness had something to do with the summery sounds and sights of bees busy in the flowers and butterflies drifting past. By the time they had reached their destination, it felt like they had left the unpleasantness of James, the theft and the crowds of tourists far behind. There were so few people at the villa right now that, for long stretches of time, they could wander in peace and admire the beautiful, old house and its breath-taking views.

Mika was enchanted by everything.

'I wish I'd known we were coming here. The brochure doesn't tell me nearly enough—just that it was built by a Swedish physician, Alex Munthe, who came to Capri in 1885.'

'You'll have plenty of time to do some research later.'

'Mmm… Oh I love this quote…' Mika's eyes were shining. 'He said, "My house must be open to the sun, to the wind and the voice of the sea, just like a Greek temple, and light, light, light everywhere". Isn't that just how it makes you feel?'

It was impossible not to smile back. Not to be drawn into the joy Mika was sharing.

'We've got it all today, haven't we? The sun and the wind. I can't hear the sea yet, though.'

'You can see it from almost every window. And, if you can see it, you can hear it. In here...' Mika touched Raoul's chest, laying her hand over his heart. 'It's a song. The most beautiful music ever...'

He put his hand over hers, dipping his head so that his forehead rested on her hair. He knew exactly what she meant and the connection between them had never felt so strong.

Maybe they'd both been born with dolphin blood in their veins...

He could smell the scent of the shampoo she used, something lemony and fresh. And, more than that, he could smell a scent that was unique to Mika. Something sweet but with a hint of spice. Something he knew he would never smell on anyone else.

Something he would never, ever forget.

They got lost wandering from room to room when they were finally ready to explore outside.

One room was the biggest yet.

'It's like a ballroom,' Mika breathed. Her gaze snagged his. 'Let's pretend…'

'Pretend what?'

'That this is our house. That there's a small orchestra just over there and they're playing music, just for us…' Her eyes shone. 'I'm wearing a dress…a really pretty, swirly dress… Dance with me, Rafe…'

She held up her arms like a child asking to be cuddled and there was no way he could refuse the request. And then he started moving. It was obvious Mika had never had the kind of formal dance instruction that he'd had but she was so easy to lead and so astonishingly light on her feet. Even without music, this was a dance he would remember. And maybe they did have music…that song that came from the voice of the sea…

It was Mika who stopped the dance. She pulled away, holding only his hand as she took one more look around them.

'Imagine *really* living somewhere like this,' she whispered. 'How unreal would that be?'

Raoul didn't have to imagine. Many elements of this wonderful old house were very similar to the palace he would soon be returning to, like the intricately tiled floors, Grecian columns and works of art that could grace any museum. His home had a ballroom much larger than this, with an area that could seat an entire orchestra. That the idea of living in such opulence was a fairy-tale for Mika drove home the realisation that he'd been avoiding for so long.

She didn't belong in any part of his world. Even wearing a pretty dress was the stuff of make-believe and that was only a tiny piece of the jigsaw that made up the lives of the people in that world.

The thought was unbearably sad. How could he leave her behind when he couldn't imagine not having her in his life now?

But how could he *not* leave her behind?

Raoul's love for his country and his grandparents was bone-deep. His destiny was already written and it included a marriage that would bring two small kingdoms together and make them both stronger, which would be of great benefit to the people he was about to take responsibility for. He couldn't walk away from any of that. He didn't want to walk away from it but...

But doing so was going to hurt them both.

He could cope. He had to. But to hurt Mika so much?

He wasn't sure he *could* do that.

A few days or weeks were nothing in the timeframe of a lifetime. How could snatching this gift of something so perfect have become such a dilemma?

He'd felt his heart crack once before when she'd touched it in an unexpected way and it felt as though that crack was widening with every gasp of astonishment or pleasure that escaped Mika as they kept exploring.

Hand in hand, they walked along the paved pathway beneath vine-covered pergolas supported by columns with splashes of vibrant colour from the flowers in perfectly manicured gardens on either side.

Their path led them past a granite sphinx that Mika had to touch, and that was the moment that Raoul felt that crack in his heart start to bleed.

Such small, clever hands. Such a light, reverent touch—as if she was still dancing.

That made sense. She was dancing her way through her life like some kind of magical creature.

He knew what it was like to be touched by those hands. How it made him feel like he was the best man he could ever be. He'd learned so much about himself in the last few weeks and it was too bound up in how he felt about Mika for the fragments ever to be separated.

When he left Mika behind, was he also going to leave behind the part of himself she'd helped him discover?

They came to a circular viewing point with an uninterrupted panorama of the Bay of Naples.

'You can see for ever,' Mika said in awe. 'I bet you can see *Les Iles Dauphins* if you look hard enough.'

Raoul stood behind Mika because he could see perfectly well over the top of her head. She leaned back against him and he put his arms around her, his breath escaping in a long sigh.

He would certainly be leaving a part of himself with Mika. A large part of his heart. But he had to believe he wouldn't lose what she had taught him. He'd learned things that were ingrained in his soul now. Things about love. Things about life. They would serve him well in the future and he would be a king that his people would be proud of.

Gazing out to the sea and the islands he knew were out there gave Raoul a pang of homesickness and, in that instant, he knew he was finally ready.

It was time he stepped back into his life.

And that meant that any reprieve was over. It was time to tell Mika the truth.

He tried to find a way to begin as they walked back to meet their boat but the words turned themselves over and over in his head and, whenever he caught Mika's gaze, they became an incomprehensible jumble.

It would be better to do it when they got back to her room, he decided. That way he could at least slip away and give her privacy to deal with the shock. How awful would it be for both of them to have to face heartbreak in public?

And it was *so* public. The crowds seemed to have swelled so much it was difficult to navigate through them to get to the train and down to the marina. Whatever celebrities had come to Capri today had certainly caused a stir. There were paparazzi everywhere, and James wasn't the only one on their return trip to Positano. He was still snapping photos. Raoul pulled the brim of the baseball cap he had been using as a sunhat further down his forehead and pushed his dark glasses further up his nose. It was probably Mika that the sleaze was trying to get a picture of but it was making him extremely uncomfortable.

Was this the kind of guy that would step in to fill the gap in her life when he had gone?

The dilemma was doing his head in.

On the one side was his duty that he could never walk away from.

On the other was his love for Mika and the overwhelming desire to be the man he was when he was with her.

There had to be a way through this that wouldn't destroy them.

And maybe there was...

Crazy thoughts were coming out of the turmoil in his head and his heart. He wasn't married yet. He wasn't even formally engaged, although the whole world was expecting the announcement. Would Francesca still *want* to marry him if she knew that his heart was with someone else?

His grandparents adored each other. Wouldn't they be prepared to allow him the same happiness of being married to the one he loved?

He needed more time to think.

Positano seemed to be as popular as Capri for tourists today and, oddly, the *Pane Quotidiano* seemed to be the most popular café. From the end of the street, it looked as if there was a crowd of people queuing to get in.

'What's going on?' Mika sounded worried. 'Maybe we should see if Marco needs extra help. They'll never be coping with that kind of crowd.'

As they got closer, the hairs on the back of Raoul's neck started to rise. He could see the cameras and he knew exactly who all these people were. A glance over his shoulder and he could see James a step or two behind them, and that was when he knew the game was up.

It was too late to try and escape. Mika was holding his hand—obliviously leading him further and further into enemy territory. He could feel her grip tighten as she realised that something unusual was going on. It was normal enough to see Marco waving his arms in the air as he spoke, but for Gianni to be out on the street as well, holding a newspaper? Other staff were filling the doorway, too, watching what was going on—Alain, the barista, and probably all the waitresses working today.

They were easily close enough to hear Marco now.

'He's *not* here. And how many times do I have to tell you that you're barking up the wrong tree? Go away—you're scaring off my customers.'

And then he spotted Mika.

'She'll tell you. *She* knows... He's her boyfriend, for heaven's sake.'

They moved as a pack, shifting their attention, lifting their cameras. Raoul could feel Mika's whole body stiffen as she froze. He could see the fear in her eyes as she looked up at him.

'*Prince Raoul...*' a dozen or more voices shouted in the instant the flashes started exploding around them. 'Look *this* way...'

CHAPTER NINE

NONE OF THIS made any sense.

Blinded by the bright flashes going off right in her face, Mika clung to Rafe's hand. He was pulling her away but her legs wouldn't co-operate. The roaring sound around them was starting to coalesce into recognisable words but it still didn't make any sense.

'*Why?*'

'Crown Prince of *Les Iles Dauphins*...'

'Washing *dishes*...?'

'Who's the girl, Prince Raoul?'

'Does your fiancée know?'

That did it. Like having a bucket of icy water thrown over her head. The word settled into Mika's consciousness and ricocheted around, inside her skull, like a bullet.

Fiancée...fiancée...fiancée...

She ripped her hand from Rafe's grip.

Rafe? Oh, yeah...he'd stumbled over the

name when he'd introduced himself, hadn't he? Up there on the Footpath of the Gods, when he'd rescued her. Some instinct had suggested that maybe he didn't want her to know his real name. Who he really was.

But…a *prince*…?

With a *fiancée*…?

She was free of his touch now. The pack of paparazzi was moving in from all sides but Mika was small.

And as hard as nails. It was easy to launch herself at a gap between two of these men, squeeze through and then start running. She didn't realise she was holding her breath until she'd almost reached the end of the street and had to stop, doubled over as her lungs screamed for some oxygen.

Turning her head, she could see that Rafe was coming after her—getting away from the crowd that had now attracted a police presence—but he'd been ambushed by someone further up the street. A slim figure wearing tight, black jeans and a tee shirt…

James?

Her world had turned upside down and Mika had to find safety. Her lungs burning, she started running again and didn't stop until she got to the boarding house and into her room, where she could slam the door behind her and push the bolt into its slot to lock it.

Now what?

Should she throw herself onto her bed and hide her face in her pillow?

The bed that she had been sharing with the man she loved so much...who wasn't the man she'd thought he was...

Should she sink onto the couch and put her face in her hands?

The couch that she'd offered to someone whom she had believed had lost everything and had no money and no place to sleep.

Oh...there was humiliation to be discovered amongst this shock.

If it was true...

But how *could* it be true?

Why would a prince pretend to be nobody? To take on an unskilled, underpaid, physically hard job and work amongst people like herself?

Why would he have chosen to *be* with someone like herself—in the most intimate way it was possible to be with someone?

Instead of choosing either the bed or the couch, Mika stayed exactly where she was, standing in the middle of her small, dingy room. She wrapped her arms tightly around herself and, instead of hiding her face, she stared at the blank wall.

His last job had been as a helicopter pilot.

She'd thought that was as unlikely as him being an astronaut or a brain surgeon.

A huff of something like laughter escaped her throat.

Why hadn't *'prince'* been at the top of that list?

And he hadn't really chosen to be with her, had he?

He'd been determined not to be. Now she could see that hesitation on his part, when she'd believed he had been about to kiss her for the first time in the valley of the mills, in a whole new light.

She'd forced him into it.

She'd *begged* him to make love to her.

Shame was a step down from humiliation. Who knew?

No wonder he hadn't wanted her to ask too many questions. He'd known all along that there was no possibility of any future for them. He'd wanted to have this time *just for them*…

Just for him, more likely. A final fling before he got married.

A bit of...*rough*?

The rattle of her door handle, swiftly followed by a sharp rap on the door, made Mika flinch.

The sound of Rafe's voice sent a spear of pain in its wake.

'Mika?' Her name was a command. 'Let me in. *Now...*'

Things had hit the fan in an astonishingly spectacular way.

The last way Raoul would have chosen.

It would have been bad enough that his identity had been revealed before he'd had the chance to tell Mika the truth but never in a million years could he have imagined how much worse it could actually be.

Clutched in his hand was a copy of the newspaper that James had shoved in his face when he'd stepped out in front of him.

The front page of a national evening paper that had the provocative headline *Prince in Hiding* and a huge photograph.

A photograph he had no idea had been taken and could have only been taken by one person.

Mika.

He remembered the moment. Standing there

on the flagged terrace in front of Bernie's bar in Praiano, watching that glorious sunset. After that swim with Mika, sitting on the pontoon and feeling that first, heady realisation that he'd found someone with whom he had an extraordinary kind of connection. He was staring out to sea, with one hand shading his eyes and clearly deeply in thought. With no sunglasses on and his beard still in the early days of its growth, it was no wonder that someone had recognised him.

How much had James been paid for that picture?

How much of a percentage had he offered Mika?

He'd been so smug.

'Say thanks to your girlfriend for me. Here— have this as a memento...'

He'd shaken off the rest of the paparazzi but it wouldn't take them long to run them down. His cover was blown and Mika's life was about to turn into a circus.

But maybe she deserved it...

Raoul banged his fist on the door again.

He'd been betrayed. And he was angry.

'Open the door, Mika. You owe me an explanation.'

The door flew open a second later.

'I owe *you* an explanation?'

Raoul unravelled the newspaper and held it in front of her.

'*You* took this picture, didn't you?'

He'd never seen her look this shocked. Not even in those first few minutes of knowing her, when she'd been in fear of her life on the side of that cliff. Or when she'd been threatened by those men intent on rape.

'How did *that* happen? Oh, my God…it was on my camera…'

For a heartbeat, he believed her. He *wanted* to believe her. But he could see the smirk on James' face as he'd asked him to pass on his thanks. And he knew how well a lot of women could act. They could make men believe whatever they wanted them to believe—especially when they had eyes like Mika. He'd believed everything she'd told him.

Had trusted her.

And she'd betrayed him. He caught hold of that anger again, like a shield.

'The camera that got so conveniently stolen.' Raoul pushed his way into the room, forcing Mika to back up, slamming the door closed behind him with his foot. 'It must have made a great cover, being jostled in that crowd on the train.'

'What on earth are you talking about?'

'You handed it over, didn't you? To your new friend *James*. Did you decide that being a travel writer wasn't a fast enough way to get to fame and fortune? Did you realise you had a much quicker route right at your fingertips?'

'You think I was *responsible* for this?'

'He told you that you could make big money if you hung out with him for the day, didn't he?'

Raoul could imagine all too easily what had really been said in that conversation.

'You think a movie star is a big deal? Boy, have I got a story—and photo—that you'd kill for...'

'What is it?'

'Hang on. Let's talk money first...'

Mika was looking stunned rather than shocked now. They hadn't lost the ability to communicate in the space of a single, sharp glance.

She was as angry as he was now.

'Why the hell would I have done that? When I didn't have the slightest idea who you actually were?

'Didn't you? *Really?* Not even when I told you where I came from?'

Raoul remembered that chill he'd felt when he'd told her the name of his homeland—the fear that she might have guessed the truth.

Had she just been waiting for an opportune moment to use that knowledge to change her life?

That was what was so much worse than everything hitting the fan.

He'd been taken for a fool.

He'd believed that Mika was in love with him for who he was as a man and not as a prince.

'I don't believe this. *I'm* the one who should be angry here. *You're* the one who lied to me.' There was a flash of something stronger than anger in her eyes now. Something like despair. 'And you said you never would...'

'I didn't lie to you.' Anger was a great way to obliterate anything like misgivings. 'I just didn't tell you who I was. I didn't *have* to, did I?'

'I didn't give that photograph to James. Even if I *had* known who you were, I would never do something like that.'

'I saw the way you looked at each other.' He'd seen it when she was back by his side on the boat and she'd turned to look at James. 'I saw the way he smiled at you. It's obvious that the deal had been done. That the arrangements for a handover were in place.'

Mika gave an incredulous huff, stepping further away from him.

'And you didn't want to go to the police, did you? I wonder why that was?'

He'd thought it was because she'd sensed his own reluctance, but now the new explanation was too obvious to ignore.

'It's not the first time this has happened,' he snapped. 'Tell me, is it easy for girls to pretend they're in love in order to get what they really want?'

Mika's face looked as if it had been carved out of stone and her voice was chillingly quiet.

'Get out,' she said. 'Get out of my life, Rafe. Or should that be *Raoul*?'

The chill of her voice and the stare he was receiving cut through the anger just enough for something else to surface.

A wash of something that felt ridiculously like…fear.

This was it, wasn't it? The last time he would ever see this woman.

And it made no difference what she'd done. He would still be leaving his heart behind.

A part of himself that he might never find again.

He did have to go, however. He could hear noises on the street below. He had to get out—probably via the fire escape—and then get himself out of sight. Summon whatever assistance he needed to get back to where he belonged. There was far too much more fallout to come from this and he had to front up and deal with it as soon as possible.

He owed his grandparents that much.

He owed his people that much.

Raoul turned. With a flick of his hand he threw the newspaper onto Mika's bed. The bed he'd been sharing with her. A symbol of just how much trouble he'd heaped on himself and those he loved.

Mika spoke as he let himself out of the room and the words followed him like an icy draft as he headed for the fire escape at the back of the old building.

'It's happened to me before, too, you know. Men pretending to be in love with me in order to get what *they* want.'

The slam of the door behind him came a split second after her final words.

'Never again.'

CHAPTER TEN

NO COMMENT...

How often had Mika used those words in the last few days?

What a nightmare.

Rafe...no, *Raoul*...had been sucked out of her life in an instant and the void had been filled by a crowd of ugly strangers who had no respect for her privacy. They wanted photographs of, and interviews with, the girl who had been the constant companion of a prince who had been hiding from the world.

That dreadful first night—and the whole of the next day—Mika had been too terrified to leave the safety of her locked room. She had never felt so alone and so scared. So utterly devastated.

A broken heart should be the least of her worries. She had undoubtedly lost her job and she couldn't even try to find another one. Not in this town, anyway. Probably not anywhere in Europe. New Zealand would be the best place to hide, but how on earth could she get there? It was half a world away and travel was expensive. She'd spent all her savings on that camera and barely had enough to meet this week's rent.

The camera that Rafe thought she'd sold. Yes…he would always be *Rafe* in her head. And her heart. The man she'd fallen in love with. Not a fairy-tale prince who couldn't exist in her world.

Did he really believe that she'd sold *him* as well?

That hurt so much that her precarious financial situation seemed to pale in comparison for long stretches of time. Time when, with the spotlight of despair, she could understand why he'd believed that. She could look back on that encounter with James from his point of view and see exactly how the shreds of evidence had come together in a way that made it look as if she'd betrayed him.

And she *had* taken that photograph. Secretly. Thinking that she might need a memento of a very special time in her life.

What a joke… There were a thousand images of Prince Raoul de Poitier on the internet.

Pictures of him in his military dress uniform with a red jacket, a row of medals and a sword hanging by his side. Formal pictures that probably hung in gilded frames in his palace. There were less formal ones of him in his flight uniform at the controls of a helicopter and some with him in a suit, performing royal duties, like opening a new museum. And there were way too many of him in immaculate evening dress with a beautiful woman by his side.

Tall, blonde women in designer gowns who clung to his arm and looked up at him, smiling, as if they'd never been so much in love. Like his *fiancée*, Princess Francesca…

His *almost* fiancée, her heart whispered.

As if it made any difference, her mind answered. It was a done deal. And this Francesca was precisely the sort of woman the world expected this prince to wed.

Besides, none of those pictures was of Rafe. The smoothly shaved man with impeccable hair was nothing like the tousled, bearded stranger she'd met on the Footpath of the Gods that day. And maybe that was something that would give her some comfort one day. None of those beautiful, polished women knew this prince the way she had.

Even if she had been nothing more than a holiday fling, he *had* loved her, she was sure of it.

Not that anyone else would ever know.

Mika had read the articles that had been splashed everywhere in the media frenzy. What a shock it had been to see her name in print. She had been a friend, apparently. A friend who'd reached out to him when he'd needed help, having lost his wallet and other possessions. A friend who'd helped him find employment and shown him what it was like to live in the kind of world a prince never really got to experience.

They must have excellent media consultants on those islands, Mika decided. The spin that this prince's heart was so much with his people that he'd actually wanted to experience the kind of hardship that many people dealt with in their lives had turned him from a spoilt royal looking for escapism into some kind of hero.

A prince of the people who would very soon become their beloved King.

And she was who she'd always been and always would be. An ordinary person. Someone who'd been a *friend*. Nothing more...

But she had been more. And, like the secret they had shared during that first meal together—that what had made the day so memorable had been that crippling episode of vertigo—there was silent communication to be found in things that she read as well. The prince's personal history was revisited again and again. She saw pictures of the stoic little boy standing beside his grandparents when his parents were being laid to rest after the tragic plane crash that had claimed their lives, and it made her heart ache for him.

They both knew what it was like to grow up without their parents and Mika could actually feel what the glance between them would always have been like—if they'd stayed together—as they acknowledged that bond again and again. At Christmas time, perhaps. Or when they saw a young mother holding the hand of her small child. Maybe he had been luckier than her, in that he'd had loving grandparents to raise him, but how hard would it have been for a boy to grow up without his father as a role model and advisor?

It had been bad enough for her. She'd never met her father—had no idea what he even looked like—and it felt like a part of herself had always been missing. If he had known she existed, would he have come to find her? Looked after her? Given her a safe place to live and loved her, even?

Given her a place to call home?

Mika could understand why Rafe had had to leave as soon as his true identity had been revealed. She could understand how he had been convinced that she'd betrayed him.

What she couldn't understand was how he hadn't realised how wrong he was as soon as he'd had time to think about it. Time to remember exactly what things had been like when they'd been together.

How much she had trusted him.

Loved him…

They had been so, so much more than merely *friends*. And they had been, ever since the moment they'd met. Had she given him her heart, without even realising it, in the instant she'd taken his hand up there on that mountain track? Had he given her at least a part of his, in that same instant? Even when he'd known it was something forbidden?

They'd both denied the physical attraction, hadn't they? They'd been fighting it for very different reasons but the barrier had been huge for them both and it had taken something traumatic to push them past the point of no return.

And Rafe had wanted it to continue as much as she had. She'd joked about him being a politician because he didn't want to give her a straight answer to her questions. He had wanted that time *just for them*…

Because he'd known it had to end the moment she knew the truth.

That was what hurt the most. That he'd taken her heart and soul *knowing* that he was going to destroy her in the near future. How could you do that, if you really loved somebody?

Had he been trying to protect himself from further scandal by dismissing their relationship as no more than friendship?

There was a part of her that refused to suffocate under the weight of betrayal. The part that would always love Rafe. It had a tiny voice but it made itself heard occasionally during the cacophony of heartbreak. It told her that he *had* loved her. So much that he couldn't bring himself to hurt her by telling her the truth. And that dismissing that love in public was the only way he had now to try and protect her.

If that was the case, it was working. Slowly. The number of paparazzi was dwindling as the days passed and her best friend amongst the waitresses—Bianca—had come to knock on her door one evening.

'You can come back to work,' she told Mika.

'Really? Has the crowd gone?'

'There's a new crowd now. People who want to see where a prince was working. Business has never been so good.'

'Marco wouldn't have me back. I didn't even tell him I was taking time off.'

'He knows why. We barely got to serve anyone apart from the journalists for a few days, anyway. And I think Marco likes being so famous. He's still sitting at his table all day, every day, happy to have his photo taken and talk to everyone.'

'I don't want to have my photograph taken. I haven't even been for a swim for days because I'm too scared to go out there. I'm terrified someone's going to be outside my door whenever I go to the bathroom. They shout at me from the street but I'm not going to give any interviews, no matter how much money I get offered.'

'They're offering you money?'

'Huge money. If I told them that we'd been sleeping together, I could probably buy a house.'

Mika's eyes filled with tears. 'But I wouldn't do that. I couldn't…'

'You really loved him, didn't you?' Bianca drew her into a hug. 'Oh, hon…'

Mika drew back from the embrace with a sigh. 'You do need money, though. What are you eating?'

'I had some cans of stuff. And coffee. I've almost run out, now, though.'

'So come back to work. Not front of house yet—that's the message I was told to give you.' Bianca's smile was wry. 'Marco probably doesn't want to share the spotlight. But he says you can have Rafe's old job, if you want. We're all having to take turns washing dishes at the moment and nobody's very happy about it.'

There really wasn't a choice to make. Mika was going to be in serious trouble if she didn't start earning a wage but how ironic would that be—to take Rafe's old job?

How much more miserable was it possible to become?

Quite a lot, it seemed.

Sneaking around to get in and back from the restaurant and avoid being seen was horrible. Not being able to go swimming was even worse. The job itself was unpleasant and back-breaking but Mika fronted up to do it day after day. It became automatic and gave her mind far too much time to wander.

To remember things that made her feel so stupid. Like sharing her dream of becoming something as important as a travel writer. Or suggesting to Rafe that they pretended they were living in the villa that was as close to a palace as she'd ever been inside. Things that made her so sad, too. Like the conviction that giving her heart to Rafe would be worth it even if he disappeared because she would always know how perfect life could be.

It didn't help at all now because Mika knew that her life could never, ever be that perfect again.

Her whole body ached.

Her heart was splintered. Nothing could ever put that many broken shards back together again.

Even her belly ached. So much that it made her feel sick sometimes. One day, Bianca brought in a load of plates that had congealed egg and bacon rinds on it and Mika took one look and had to flee to the toilet to throw up.

She was splashing cold water on her face when Bianca slipped into the tiny restroom and closed the door behind her.

She met Mika's gaze in the spotted mirror above the hand basin and her eyes were troubled.

'Are you in trouble, hon?'

'What do you mean?'

'Are you pregnant?'

'*No.*' The thought was so shocking, Mika had to grip the sides of the basin to persuade her legs to keep holding her up.

'Is it possible?'

Was it? Her mind flew back to that silent conversation in the pharmacy that night.

Is it too late?

It was a safe time, I'm sure of it.

But how long ago had that been?

Weeks…

Way *too* long…

'Oh, my God…'

The basin wasn't enough support any more. Mika's shoulder was already against the wall of the tiny room. She leaned against it as she let herself slide to the floor where she could curl up, hug her knees and hide her face by resting it on her arms.

She would have to ask Bianca to go to the pharmacy and buy a test kit for her to avoid attracting the attention of any lurking journalists but Mika already knew what the answer was going to be.

It would be better, in fact, if she went somewhere else to do it herself so that her friend wouldn't be involved. Somewhere a long way from here where nobody would recognise her as being the 'friend' of the prince. She couldn't afford to go back to New Zealand but there were a lot of big cities in Europe that she could hide in. A train ticket wouldn't be expensive and she could carry everything she owned in a backpack, couldn't she? If she sold her laptop, that would not only give her enough money, it would make the backpack lighter to carry.

The thought of being so totally alone was terrifying. The prospect of facing it came with a wave of dizziness that reminded her of the moment she had realised she was in so much trouble on that mountain track.

The day that Rafe had come into her life...

As impossible as it might have seemed, her heart broke a little more.

Had she really thought that working as a

dish washer would be the most miserable extra change in her life now?

How wrong had she been?

CHAPTER ELEVEN

PRINCE RAOUL DE POITIER was standing in front of his bathroom mirror. A gilt-framed mirror that reflected just how completely the circumstances of his life had returned to normal. How different was this to the shared facilities of that boarding house, with the vastness of the private room, its generous showering and bathing facilities, countless soft, fluffy towels and a selection of skin products any pharmacy would be proud to display?

The aftershave he'd just splashed on his face still stung even though the beard was long gone. How long would it take for his skin to stop feeling oddly raw and exposed?

His heart still felt raw, too.

Unbelievably heavy.

And he didn't like the man he was staring at in the mirror.

His journey of self-discovery had been a disaster. He'd learned something that he wasn't sure he could live with.

That he was a man who could take someone's heart and then crush it for the greater good of others.

Had he really believed—in his heart—that Mika had sold that picture and betrayed his identity? That she knew she'd fallen in love with a prince?

Of course she hadn't. She had fallen in love with the man she believed him to be. An ordinary bloke by the name of Rafe.

He'd let his mind overrule his heart in that instant. Allowed himself to feel betrayed and then angry because that was the easiest escape route as the reprieve of an ordinary life had exploded around him.

He'd left Mika believing that he'd simply used her.

That he hadn't really loved her.

And she deserved so much more than that.

But what could he do?

His duty.

As he had been doing ever since he'd been whisked back to *Les Iles Dauphins*, away from the media circus in Positano. The look of shock on the faces of his grandparents when he'd walked into the palace with his long hair and beard, wearing his shorts and the 'I heart Positano' tee shirt had told him just how far past acceptable boundaries he had wandered. The days that followed had been a matter of damage control and, thanks to a quick-thinking team of media experts and the unwavering support of his grandparents, what could have been a complete scandal had been turned around to make him some kind of hero.

A man of the people who, thanks to a courageous action, now knew exactly what it was like to be an ordinary person. He was someone who understood them and whom they could trust to rule them with compassion and wisdom.

But Raoul would never feel like a hero.

He had a million images of Mika imprinted on his mind and in his heart, but the only one he could hold in his hand was the one taken in that dreadful moment they'd been spotted at *Pane Quotidiano*. She had been wearing that white singlet top that was his favourite, because it showed off her gorgeous brown skin and revealed the tattoo that was a symbol of the sea that meant so much to her.

Dolphin blood…

The voice of the sea…

The way he could dance with her with only the music in their hearts to follow…

The mosaic tiles of his bathroom floor were not unlike the surface they had danced on in that old villa.

The house that Mika had thought a palace.

That she'd wanted to pretend to be living in. With him…

Dear Lord…he'd never known how much it was possible to miss someone.

Or maybe he had and that was why this was so difficult. It took him back to being that scared five-year-old, standing so stoically during the final farewell to his parents.

Doing his duty, even then, because he knew what was expected of him by so many people.

And today, he was about to take his next step into doing what was expected of him. Francesca was due to arrive later. It was time to propose. To make the engagement official. His mother's ring was in a velvet case on his dressing table, waiting for him to slip it into his pocket. There would be a celebratory lunch and many, many photographs to go with the press release. There would also be the first of what would probably be many, many meetings to arrange their wedding—a train of events that there would be no possibility of stopping once it had begun.

The sensation of a ticking clock had never been so strong. He had to do something before it was too late. Something that would, at least, give Mika the comfort of knowing that he cared.

That he was truly sorry.

One of his personal assistants had his suit ready for him when he left the bathroom suite that adjoined his bedroom.

'Their Royal Highnesses are taking breakfast in their suite,' he was informed. 'They would like you to join them.'

'Of course.' Raoul donned the crisp, white shirt and held out his wrists to have the cufflinks inserted. His favourite ones, which were gold, embossed with the image of a leaping dolphin.

His heart grew even heavier. It was like a very personal punishment that the symbol of his homeland was going to remind him of Mika every day for the rest of his life.

'Pierre?'

'Yes, sir?'

'I have a task for you this morning. I want

you to source a camera. A Nikon D4—or something better if there's a new model available.'

'Certainly.'

Pierre was his most trusted assistant. Raoul would have described him almost as a friend, except that he now knew what real friendship felt like.

What true love felt like…

Pierre held out his jacket so that he could slip his arms inside the silk lining. 'Are you becoming interested in taking up photography?'

'No. It's a gift. I want you to buy a range of lenses to go with it, too. And any other accessories that are recommended. And I want everything in a case. Gift-wrapped.'

'No problem. Would you like me to arrange delivery, as well?'

'Not yet. I need to think about that. It will need discretion.'

Pierre didn't bat an eyelash. 'Just let me know, then, Sir. I'm sure something can be arranged.'

The palace of *Les Iles Dauphins* was on a headland that gave it sweeping views of the Mediterranean and the suite of rooms that was his grandparents' private domain had a terrace with the best view of all because you could see the royal beach—a tiny, private bay that could only be reached via the stone staircase from the palace gardens.

On a beautiful morning like this, the only thing that could disturb the clear blue of the calm water was the way the bay's permanent residents greeted a new day. The joyful leaping of the small pod of dolphins that claimed this well-protected bay as their home base was such a pleasure to watch, it was no wonder that this was the preferred spot for Prince Henri II and his wife, Gisele, to take their breakfast.

There was something about the scene on the terrace that made Raoul pause for a moment before he joined them. His grandparents, as always, were sitting close together on both sides of a corner. At this particular moment, they weren't eating or admiring the view, they were looking at each other. Smiling.

The heavy lump that was Raoul's heart this morning twisted a little in his chest. He loved these people—his family—so much. And he loved that they still loved each other, after so many decades of being together. Remembering that they were both well into their eighties now was a poignant reminder that their time was limited, and as Raoul moved close enough to bestow his customary kiss on the soft skin of his grandmother's cheek he made a silent vow to make the rest of that time as perfect as possible.

They had given him so much.

'Good morning, Mamé... Papé.' The child-ish names for his grandparents had never been relinquished in private. 'It's a beautiful day, isn't it?'

'Help yourself, darling.' Gisele waved at the covered platters on the serving table behind them. 'I ordered your favourite cheese and mushroom omelette.'

'Can I get you something? More coffee?'

'Some orange juice for Henri, perhaps. He hasn't taken all his pills yet.'

His grandfather made a grumbling sound that suggested he didn't need to be nagged but he winked at Raoul.

'Big day for you, today,' he said. 'What time does the beautiful Francesca arrive?'

'Late this morning.'

'There's a formal luncheon,' Gisele added. 'And photographs this afternoon. It's in your diary, Henri.'

Raoul put the plate with its fluffy omelette

and pretty roasted tomatoes in front of him at the table. He picked up his fork but then put it down again. He really wasn't hungry. He sipped his coffee, instead, and watched as his grandmother arranged the morning medication for his grandfather, handing over each pill and watching carefully as it was taken. It was impossible not to notice the tremor in his grandfather's hand and the way Gisele put each tablet into his palm with enough care that it wouldn't be dropped.

'Is there something wrong with the omelette, Raoul?'

'No, Mamé. It's perfect. I'm just not very hungry.'

'But you're losing weight. You haven't been like yourself ever since you got home. I'm worried about you, darling…'

His grandfather reached out to pat her hand. 'The thought of marriage makes any man a little nervous.' He smiled at Raoul. 'Don't worry, lad. It gets better.'

But Gisele looked anxious. 'It is a big step. And so close to your coronation. Is it too soon? We haven't finalised the date. Francesca's grandmother is one of my oldest friends and I'm sure we could arrange for it to be delayed…'

Raoul saw the glance his grandparents exchanged. A delay wasn't something they wanted and he could understand why. These two had been together since before Henri had become the ruling Prince of *Les Iles Dauphins*. He had always had the loving support of his wife by his side.

They wanted the same thing for him, didn't they?

That support was something that came naturally when you loved someone. Mika could have given him that. As he would have given her...

Would delaying his marriage change how he felt?

No. It would make things worse because he'd have more time to imagine a very different future. With Mika as his princess. Sitting out here, one day in the future, having breakfast and watching dolphins play...

'What's the secret?' The question came unexpectedly. 'For a happy marriage?'

'Respect,' his grandfather said.

'Love,' His grandmother smiled.

'Were you both in love when you married?'

'In *love*?' His grandfather grunted. 'Stuff and nonsense.'

But Gisele's eyes twinkled. 'Oh, yes, we were. You couldn't keep your hands off me, Henri.'

A huff of surprised laughter escaped Raoul. 'Too much information, Mamé.' His laughter faded. 'You chose each other, though, didn't you?'

'What do you mean?'

'Your marriage wasn't arranged.'

'That's true,' Gisele murmured. 'I was his mother's secretary. It was all a bit of a scandal, really.'

'But everybody forgave you, didn't they? Because they knew how much in love you were?'

'Oh… Raoul…' Gisele's words were no more than a sigh.

A coffee cup rattled loudly as Henri tried to put it down on its saucer. 'Are you saying you don't want your marriage to go ahead?'

The coffee had spilled onto the tablecloth. His grandfather was suddenly looking older. Almost grey. Unwell…?

Raoul backed off from whatever he might have been about to say. 'Francesca is beautiful. She's already a princess. She's an ideal choice.'

'But not *your* choice.' His grandmother's faded blue eyes looked suspiciously bright. 'You're not in love with her…'

'In *love*.' Henri's words were dismissive. 'Stuff and nonsense. It's no more than lust.' The old Prince was rubbing his chest with one hand. He pushed back his chair and got to his feet, leaning on the table as he did so.

'Are you all right, Papé?' Raoul was alarmed. 'You don't have a pain in your chest, do you?'

'I'm fine. I'll see you…*and* Francesca…at luncheon.'

Raoul caught his grandmother's gaze.

'I'll go,' she said quietly. 'I'll call the doctor.' She paused to touch Raoul's head as she passed. 'It'll be all right,' she added. 'Don't worry…'

That Gisele chose to join him in what was supposed to have been a private meeting before lunch was more than a surprise to Raoul. How was he supposed to propose with an audience?

'Is something wrong? Is it Grand-père?'

His grandmother took a seat beside Francesca, opposite him, on a matching small, overstuffed couch.

'He's resting,' she said. 'The doctor thinks it was his angina. He needs to use his spray more often.' She turned to smile at Francesca. 'How are you, my dear? I've just been having such a lovely chat to your grandmother.'

'Oh?' Francesca's smile wavered.

Raoul frowned. This meeting had been going well. He and Francesca had a lot in common and, while things felt a little awkward still, they just needed more time to get to know each other better. He liked her and she seemed to like him.

They hadn't got near discussing the really important business between them but it had been a good start.

'You've done so well in your studies,' Gisele continued. 'I didn't realise how close you were to graduating as a doctor.'

Francesca bit her lip. 'I've arranged to take leave from my studies. I'm hoping I can finish them one day and, while I know I could never practise as a physician, I hope I can become involved with the health systems in both our countries.'

'It's your passion, isn't it?'

Francesca looked down at her hands. She spoke quietly. 'I've been brought up to understand my position in life and my duty—to both my family and my country. I would never do anything to harm the people I love.'

She raised her head to look at Raoul and he could see a determination that reminded him so much of Mika that he had to smile back. He could respect that.

'But what about Carlos?'

Francesca turned her head with a gasp. 'Oh…my grandmother swore she would never say anything…'

Raoul blinked. 'Who's Carlos?'

Gisele patted Francesca's hand. 'Another passion, I think.'

Francesca's eyes filled with tears as she looked back at Raoul 'I'm sorry,' she whispered. 'I would never have said anything. And it's over now. It had to be…'

Raoul's smile was gentle. 'I understand. Believe me…'

'Of course he does,' Gisele said. 'Now, I'm going to leave you two to have a talk. Just bear one thing in mind. Anything is possible.' She was smiling as she got to her feet. 'Just look at what Raoul managed to do in his time away. And how well it was handled. Everybody understands true love.'

The silence in the room grew louder as he and Francesca sat there, both more than a little stunned.

'What did she mean?' Francesca asked finally.

'I think she knows more than I realised,' Raoul admitted. 'I... I met someone while I was away.'

'You're in love with her?'

Raoul swallowed. And then nodded. He cleared his throat. 'And you're in love with... with Carlos?'

The glow in her eyes was more than enough to confirm it.

'But you were going to go ahead and do your duty and marry *me*?'

It was Francesca's turn to nod.

He had been going to do the same thing but this changed everything, didn't it?

If there was one thing that Raoul had learned from his escape from his real life, it was that he was, at heart, a good man. Someone who could love, nurture and protect. A man who could trust his instincts about what was right and wrong.

And this was wrong. Was that the message his grandmother had been trying to leave him with? That it was possible to follow his instincts? That anything could be managed and forgiven in the name of true love?

'We both have a position in life that carries a huge responsibility,' he said slowly. 'A duty to do the best for all those that we are responsible for.'

'Yes.' Francesca's head was bowed. 'I'm only twenty-five,' she whispered. 'But I feel like a parent. One with many thousands of children.'

'Have you flown anywhere recently?'

'What?' Her head jerked up. 'Of course… I flew here. What's that got to do with anything?'

'I don't mean on a private jet. I meant on an ordinary commercial flight.'

'Oh, yes. I've done that.'

'Did you watch the safety briefing?'

Francesca's eyes were wide and puzzled.

'They tell you what to do if an oxygen mask appears,' Raoul continued. 'They tell you that you should put your own on before you help others.' He took a deep breath. 'We have a duty to many people, Francesca, but we also have a duty to ourselves. To make sure that we are in the best position to do our best for others.'

'You mean…?' Her words died but he could see the birth of hope in her eyes.

'I mean that you should be with the person you love,' Raoul said softly. 'And so should I…'

The private helicopter with its royal insignia touched down in Positano late that afternoon.

Carrying the heavy, beautifully wrapped parcel, Raoul and his bodyguards made their way as discreetly as possible to the *Pane Quotidiano*.

Marco was sitting at his usual table on the pavement His jaw dropped when he saw the group approaching.

'I've come to see Mika,' Raoul told him. 'I… have something for her.'

'She's…ah…she's not here.'

Others had noticed his arrival. Bianca came outside.

'She's gone,' she told Raoul.

'Where?'

'I don't know.' Bianca shook her head. 'She just vanished. Days ago. I went to her room when she didn't show up one day but it's empty. She's gone…' She touched Raoul's arm. 'You have to find her,' she said quietly. 'It's important.'

CHAPTER TWELVE

IT WAS A fairy-tale palace.With tall stone walls and turrets and spires that were becoming a dramatic silhouette as the blinding sunshine of the day began to fade.

With her dark sunglasses, a big, floppy hat on her head and the backpack over her shoulders, Mika knew she passed as any ordinary tourist who'd come to these remote islands.

Someone who even advertised her love for the creatures this land was named for by wearing a tiny, silver replica around her neck.

She had walked up a big hill from the marina where her ferry had docked and she hadn't needed a map to find her destination. She might have sold her laptop but it had been easy to find an internet café, in the village where she'd been lying low for the last week or so. She'd done her research as thoroughly as she always did and the route to the de Poitier Palace was imprinted on her mind.

So was another email she had received. One that had given her confidence to face a new future. The *National Geographic* not only wanted to buy both her articles, they wanted more…

She could do this.

She could support not only herself but the baby she was going to bring into the world.

What she couldn't do was repeat the mistakes of the past.

Her baby was not going to grow up with no idea of who its father was. Not knowing a land where so many generations of his family had come from. He—or she—was never going to feel abandoned. Or unwanted.

This baby was going to be loved. And cared for and protected.

And that was what had finally given Mika the courage to make this journey.

Her father had never known she existed, so he'd never had the chance to fill even a tiny part of the gap that had been left in her life.

In a way, Mika was doing this for herself—to put right a past wrong. She was doing it for her baby, too, of course. And she was doing it for Rafe. He had the right to know that he was going to be a father. And, because she had no intention of hiding the truth from her child as it grew old enough to understand, the royal family deserved the courtesy of a warning.

It would cause a scandal one day, but maybe, with enough time to prepare for it, something could be arranged to protect the small, illegitimate prince or princess who was going to be born.

Mika had no idea how that might be done.

Now that she was here, she had no idea of what to do next. How did one go about asking to speak to a prince? She was just an ordinary tourist, standing here outside the palace, gazing through the enormous, wrought-iron gates. A rather wilted tourist. It had been such a hot day and a long walk up a decidedly steep hill.

The sound of an approaching helicopter made her look up. The sound grew louder and louder as the helicopter circled and came lower, finally disappearing on the other side of the palace where, presumably, there was a heliport.

Was Rafe at the controls?

Mika's heart skipped a beat and then sped up.

If she stood here long enough, would a guard of some kind come and ask her what she wanted? There had to be people watching. Security cameras at the very least.

And, if someone did come, would they simply laugh at her request or was it possible they could pass on a message of some kind?

It wasn't possible.

Raoul had barely caught a glimpse of the figure standing outside the palace gates as his helicopter had come in to land but he had known instantly who it was.

Had he seen her with his heart instead of his eyes?

He barely registered what the voice in his headphones was telling him.

'She hasn't used her passport.' His head of security had been busy on the flight home. 'Not at an airport, anyway. So she can't have gone back to New Zealand.'

'No.' Raoul closed his eyes as the aircraft touched down gently He could still see the shape of that small figure standing there outside his home. 'I don't think she has. Don't worry about it any more, Phillipe. I can handle it now.'

Mika had come to find *him*…

Hope was filling the dark space he had entered after finding that she'd disappeared from the café in Positano.

He ducked his head to stride beneath the slowing rotors of the helicopter. He waved off his bodyguards as he avoided the nearest palace entrance. He knew there would be many eyes watching him as he ran through the gardens, only slowing as he finally reached the front of the palace, but he didn't care.

Would Mika still be there?

The turrets and spires weren't the only silhouette against the fading light. Indecision had kept Mika immobile but it seemed that her plan might be working. A guard was coming around the corner of the palace. Not someone in a military uniform that she might have expected but a tall man in a dark suit. He looked like a bodyguard. A member of some special forces, perhaps, who'd been dispatched to find out what she thought she was doing, standing here and staring for so long.

Except…there was something about the way this man was moving. And well before he got to her—when he'd only just reached a long, rectangular pond with its blaze of flowering water lilies and the fountain that was a whole pod of leaping dolphins—the massive gates in front of Mika magically began to swing open.

Inviting her in…

But she couldn't move.

Not until the figure got even closer. Until she could see the expression on Rafe's face. Until he'd taken off his sunglasses and she could see the expression in his eyes…

Even then, she couldn't move.

This was like nothing she could have prepared herself for.

Rafe didn't even know she was pregnant.

But he wanted *her*.

As much as she wanted *him*…

This was perfect.

If he'd had a magic wand to wave, this was the one place he would have chosen to bring Mika.

A place that could provide the things that she loved most in the world.

The sea.

And dolphins.

He'd done no more than take her hand as the palace gates swung shut behind them because he knew how many people were watching.

'Come with me,' was all he said.

There was no one here on the private royal beach. Oh, it was quite possible his grandmother could see them, but if she was watching she would be smiling.

Crying, perhaps. The way she had when she'd taken him aside after Francesca had gone earlier today.

'You reminded me this morning of what it was like,' she'd said. *'When Henri and I were so much in love. If this is where your heart is, Raoul, you have to follow it. You have my blessing. You'll have the blessing of your grandfather, too, when I explain. And your people...'*

Mika's backpack lay abandoned on the sand. He might have guessed she would be wearing that white bikini as her underwear. His own suit was discarded alongside the backpack. He had nothing more than his silk boxer shorts to swim in, but it didn't matter. The light was fading fast anyway and the rosy glow of the sunset made the shapes of the dolphins swimming around them dark and mysterious.

As dark as Mika's eyes as he finally pulled her into his arms and kissed her. They way he'd been dreaming of kissing her every night they'd been apart.

'I was so afraid I wouldn't be able to find

you,' he whispered, his lips still brushing hers. 'I thought I would be missing you every minute of every day for the rest of my life.'

'I'm here.' Mika was smiling against his lips. 'I had to come. There's something I have to tell you…'

That she forgave him for the accusation he'd made? That she still loved him?

A note in her voice told Raoul that it was time they talked properly. This time in the water had taken them back enough to re-establish their connection. To wash away the pain of their time apart. It wasn't the place really to talk, though.

He led her from the shallows onto the sun-warmed sand. The air around them was still warm, too, but he picked up the jacket of his suit and draped it around Mika's shoulders. And then he sat beside her and took her hand again.

'There's something I need to tell you, too.'

It felt like he was still out of his depth in the sea, looking into her eyes. As if he could drown…

'I love you, Mika. And I'm sorry.'

'For thinking I'd sold that picture? It doesn't matter.'

'I'm sorry for more than that.'

Mika ducked her head and nodded. 'I understand. I know you couldn't tell me who you were. It would have ruined everything, wouldn't it? We'd never have…' A soft sound escaped her lips. An incredulous sort of huff as she left her sentence unfinished. And then she looked up. 'You saved me, you know? Three times…'

'Three?'

'Up on the track. From those men. And… and from maybe spending the rest of my life too scared to ever trust someone. Of never finding someone to be with like that. Of never… becoming a mother…'

It took a long, long moment for the implication of those words to sink in.

When it did, it took another long moment for Raoul to find his voice.

'You're not…?'

Just a single nod and his world changed for ever.

'I'm sorry. I really did think it was a safe time. I must have got my dates mixed up…'

'And that's why you came here today? To tell me?'

Another nod. 'I want this baby to always feel

wanted. Loved. Even if we could never be together, I want it to know who its father is.'

Like Mika never had. Raoul's heart felt so full it was in danger of bursting.

'He—or she— will always feel loved,' he said softly. The wonder of it was really sinking in now. He was going to be a *father*? 'Will always *be* loved,' he added. 'So will you…'

It was a long time before they could speak again but it made no difference because the touch of their lips and bodies would always be a conversation in itself.

How had he ever thought he could live without this woman in his life? By his side?

'This is going to cause trouble, isn't it?'

'No.' Raoul pressed another gentle kiss to Mika's lips. 'It will be a cause for great celebration. My grandmother is going to be so happy. She wants nothing more than to see me settled and happy. To be married and raising a family.'

'But…what about your fiancée?'

'We were never officially engaged. And Francesca will be just as happy as we are. She's going to be with the person *she* loves. We will maintain a friendship and work together to strengthen both our countries.'

'But…'

'But what?' Raoul swallowed a sudden fear. 'Are you worried that this isn't the place that you've been searching for? That you couldn't be happy living here?'

'I've only seen a tiny part but I already know this is the most beautiful place on earth.' Mika was smiling as she looked out at the small bay, as if she could still see the beautiful creatures who had shared their swim. She turned back to Raoul. 'And you know what?'

'What?'

'I've discovered something. A place isn't a *place*.' She touched Raoul's cheek softly. 'Or it is, but it doesn't actually matter *where* it is. That place only exists because it's beside a person. You told me that, but I wasn't really listening.' Her voice sounded like it was choked with tears. 'My place in the world is beside you, Rafe. Wherever you are, if I'm beside you, I'm *home*. But…'

Raoul was blinking back tears too. Because he couldn't have put it better himself.

'But…?'

Mika shook her head. 'I can't marry you.'

Maybe the air wasn't as warm as he'd thought. The sudden chill went right to Raoul's bones.

'Why not?'

'Are you kidding? Me? A…a *princess*? It's impossible.'

'You've forgotten something else I told you, haven't you?'

'What?'

'That you can be anything at all that you really want to be. It's one of the things I adore so much about you, my love. Your courage. And your determination. You could be a princess. *If* that's what you want.'

'If it means being with you for the rest of my life, why wouldn't I want it?'

'I was afraid you would never want to be part of my world. That's another thing I love about you. That wildness. Your freedom. Your…dolphin blood. There are constraints with being royal and it might be like putting you in a cage. A gilded cage, but the walls are still there.'

'You'd be inside those walls, too.' Mika's smile was so tender, Raoul could feel his breath catch. 'It's still the place I'd always want to be. But fairy-tales don't really happen. I don't have a fairy godmother out there to wave her wand, put me in a pretty dress and let me dance away with my prince…'

'Oh, but you have.' Any fears evaporated as Raoul kissed her again. 'You just haven't met my grandmother yet…'

EPILOGUE

HER ROYAL HIGHNESS, Princess Gisele, adjusted
the folds of her dress as she settled onto the ornate, red velvet chair with its gilded arms and
headrest.

Being in this prime position at the front of
Les Iles Dauphins' historic cathedral meant that
she could take in the full majesty of the wonderful old, stone building—the ornate archways
and pillars, the glowing wood of the rows of
pews and the statues of her country's most sig-
nificant figures whose mortal remains had been
laid to rest in the raised vaults. The stained-
glass windows were renowned as well and right
now the intricate panes of glass were glowing
as they were touched by the day's fading sunshine.

It could be—and often had been—a sombre
place to sit but not today.

Today there were garlands of snowy white

flowers on every pew and around the base of every statue. There was joyful music thundering from the enormous pipes of the organ and the harmony of a choir to add to its tone. And there was a sea of colour wherever Gisele's gaze roamed. So many beautiful dresses in shades of pink, blue and mauve. So many wonderful hats on the women in the pews that gave way to tiaras and crowns towards the front of the congregation. Nobody had refused the invitation to attend this function so it was a 'who's who' of European royalty.

Only one seat was empty and that was the one right beside Gisele.

Henri's chair.

With a sigh, Gisele shifted her gaze once more and caught that of her beloved grandson. He looked every inch the Prince he was in his military uniform with its red sash and gold epaulettes. His medals shone and the silver scabbard of his sword had been polished to within an inch of its life.

Their gazes held for a long moment. This was such a happy occasion but there was sadness, too. Loved ones who couldn't be here had to be acknowledged.

The music was softer now, so it was possible to hear the faint roar coming from outside the cathedral walls. The sound of thousands of voices in a collective cheer. Gisele could imagine the scene as vividly as if she were standing out there on the top of that huge sweep of wide steps.

The ornate, gold dolphin coach that was only brought out on the most momentous of occasions—pulled by the immaculately groomed white horses of the royal stables—would have just come to a halt at the bottom of the steps.

Another man, in a uniform even more impressive than Raoul's, would alight from the open coach and would be holding out his hand to help the bride climb down.

How wonderful was it that Mika had asked Henri to be the man to escort her down the aisle today?

And what a blessing he was still well enough to do this. He seemed to have taken on a whole new lease of life, in fact, with such joy to look forward to.

He hadn't really needed Gisele to remind him of what it had been like to be young and in love. Or of how much strength that love had given them both over the decades and how it had got them through some very difficult times.

Mika had won Henri's heart so quickly.

Had won everybody's hearts.

What could have been a dreadful scandal had miraculously become the love story of the century. Raoul was now firmly ensconced as 'the People's Prince' and he had clearly found a princess worthy of ruling by his side. Not only could everybody rejoice on the occasion of a royal wedding, they still had the coronation to look forward to and—even better—the anticipation of the birth of a new prince or princess in the near future. The first member of the next generation of the de Poitier family.

So much happiness.

Gisele had a lace-edged handkerchief clutched in her hand and she had a feeling she would need to use it very soon. She could feel tears of joy gathering as the music paused and then swelled into the triumphant opening bars of Wagner's *Bridal Chorus*. She rose to her feet, as did everybody else in the cathedral.

It was beginning.

The tears started as soon as she saw her beloved husband by the side of this exquisite young bride. They continued as her heart caught at the sight of all the children following the pair. It had been Mika's idea—to go to the orphanage and choose everyone who wanted to be a flower girl or a page boy. The girls wore long white dresses and had colourful garlands of flowers on their heads and the boys looked adorable in sailor suits.

Mika looked beyond adorable. She had approached this intimidating occasion with the same kind of good-humoured determination that she was applying to every aspect of royal life she'd been learning in the last few months. The design of her dress was simple and didn't accentuate her growing bump. Mika had asked for a 'swirly' dress that would look pretty when she danced with her new husband later and the dressmakers had been delighted to oblige. With an empire line, it fell in soft folds, the beaded bodice having a sweetheart neckline.

Gisele had offered a diamond necklace to match the tiara that was holding her veil in place but Mika had been right in choosing something else.

Her own necklace of that tiny, silver dolphin charm.

The priests leading the procession up the aisle reached their positions at the front of the cathedral now and there was nothing to obstruct the lines of vision as Raoul and Mika got closer to each other.

Henri left Mika by Raoul's side and came to sit beside Gisele. Would the television cameras pick up the way their hands touched and then held? It wasn't exactly protocol on a formal occasion but Gisele needed the touch. Her heart was so full it almost hurt.

Squeezing his fingers, she watched as Raoul lifted his bride's veil back and revealed her face. And then, for a heartbeat, and then another, the bride and groom seemed to be lost in each other's eyes.

And those smiles...

Gisele had to let go of Henri's hand, then. She needed her handkerchief too much.

So much joy was simply too contagious...

* * * * *

COMING NEXT MONTH FROM

⬡ HARLEQUIN®
Romance

Available September 6, 2016

#4535 STEPPING INTO THE PRINCE'S WORLD
by Marion Lennox
Caretaker Claire Tremaine finds a handsome soldier shipwrecked on her shores, and is soon won over by his kindness and kisses. But when she learns he's the royal prince of Marétal, she's *certain* they can't be together! That is, until Prince Raoul whisks her off to his royal palace!

#4536 UNVEILING THE BRIDESMAID
by Jessica Gilmore
New York artist Gael is convinced that love is a sham. But after spending time with shy Hope McKenzie, who has thrown herself into planning her sister's wedding, he begins to wonder if this beautiful bridesmaid is what he's been missing all along...

#4537 THE CEO'S SURPRISE FAMILY
by Teresa Carpenter
When CEO Jethro Calder discovers he is a father, he doesn't believe he can be the parent his daughter needs. But to ensure that Lexi Malone—the woman caring for his daughter—is, he invites her to stay, and soon finds that happy families do exist!

#4538 THE BILLIONAIRE FROM HER PAST
by Leah Ashton
Mila Molyneux always harboured a secret crush on childhood friend Sebastian Fyfe, until he married another woman! When she meets him years later—now widowed and as gorgeous as ever—she finds their connection is still strong... Will this reunion be Mila's opportunity to tell Seb she wants more than friendship?

YOU CAN FIND MORE INFORMATION ON UPCOMING HARLEQUIN® TITLES, FREE EXCERPTS AND MORE AT WWW.HARLEQUIN.COM.

HRLPCNM0816

SPECIAL EXCERPT FROM

HARLEQUIN®

Romance

When Crown Prince Raoul is shipwrecked with Claire Tremaine, he finds himself irresistibly drawn to the guarded beauty. But what will happen when she discovers his royal secret?

Read on for a sneak preview of
STEPPING INTO THE PRINCE'S WORLD,
the spellbinding new book
from Marion Lennox.

He'd known her for less than two days. This was just a kiss.

So why did it feel as if breaking apart from her would break something inside him?

And, amazingly, she seemed to feel the same. Her body was molding to his and her hands cupped his face, deepening the kiss. She was warm and strong and wonderful, and the feel of her mouth under his was making his body desire as he'd never felt desire.

This wasn't just a kiss. It could never be just a kiss. This was the sealing of a promise that was unvoiced but seemed to have been made the moment she'd crashed into him out in the water.

Claire.

If she wanted to pull back now he'd let her. Of course he would. He must, because this was a woman to be honored.

Honor.

HREXP0816

With that thought came another, and it was a jolt of reality that left him reeling.

This woman had saved his life. She'd been injured, battered, drugged, all to save his sorry hide, and now she was sharing her place of refuge with him.

Right now he wanted her more than anything he'd ever wanted in his life, but…

But. The word was like a hammer blow in his brain.

But he was a man of honor…

A prince…

He hadn't even told her who he was. If this went further she'd wake up tomorrow and know she'd been with the heir to the throne of Marétal.

There'd be consequences, and consequences had been drilled into him since birth.

But how could he think of consequences? He was kissing Claire and she was kissing him back. How could he think past it?

How could he draw away?

Don't miss
STEPPING INTO THE PRINCE'S WORLD
by Marion Lennox,
available September 2016 wherever
Harlequin Romance books and ebooks are sold.

www.Harlequin.com

Reading Has Its Rewards

Earn **FREE BOOKS!**

Register at **Harlequin My Rewards** and submit your Harlequin purchases from wherever you shop to earn points for free books and other exclusive rewards.

Plus submit your purchases from now till May 30th for a chance to win a $500 Visa Card*.

Visit **HarlequinMyRewards.com** today

MYR16R1